MAIDEN ROCK

MAIDEN ROCK

BY

MARY LOGUE

BLEAK HOUSE BOOKS

MADISON | WISCONSIN

Published by Bleak House Books,
an imprint of Big Earth Publishing
923 Williamson St.
Madison, WI 53703

This is a work of fiction. Any similarities to people or places, living or dead, is purely coincidental.

ISBN 13 (cloth): 978-1-932557-59-6

Printed in the United States of America.

11 10 09 08 07   1 2 3 4 5

Library of Congress Cataloging-in-Publication Data has been applied for.

Set in Adobe Garamond Pro

Cover and book design by Von Bliss Design
"Book Design By Bookish People"
www.vonbliss.com

Cover photograph provided by West Wisconsin Land Trust, www.wwlt.org.

Far, far below, a depth profound,
The lake sends up a murmuring sound,
Meet place beneath the cloudless skies,
For love's last solemn sacrifice.

"Legend of Maiden Rock," anonymous

November 1, 12:01 a.m.

Her face burst into flames. Her skin split along its seams. The earth broke wide open. She looked at the sky and she was the sky. Like she was so powerful she could do anything she thought of doing.

The top of her head lifted off and the whole world swirled into it, batter into a cake pan. Every cell in her body was doing the shimmy.

It was like what she thought sex might be at its very, very best.

She stretched out in the field, falling back and back, and back, the night sky opening on top of her.

Forever.

Stars bloomed.

She'd never seen how deep the sky was, how many millions of layers it had. She'd lived in the country all her life and the sky had always seemed shut as a closet door. She wanted to stay in this moment the rest of her life, counting stars and thinking how big the universe was.

That's how it felt when she tried it for the first time. A whole new world was born. Her nose stung as if she'd inhaled lighter fluid, but her mind was running on high-octane gasoline a million miles an hour.

The two guys on either side of her were not paying any attention. They were arguing about something, their voices a nasty buzzing in her ears. She had a million questions to ask them, but couldn't be bothered to open her mouth. She knew if she did she would never stop talking.

She closed her eyes for a moment, to take it all in. Thoughts spun through her head like orbiting comets. The universe was out there and inside of her. She knew so many things she hadn't known before. Secret doors were opening.

She knew what the thin man wanted. He was after her. Weird how that happened. The boy she wanted didn't want her. Still hard for her to believe. It was why she had left the party with these other two guys, just to get away from it all.

She stood and the air lifted her up. How easy it all was. She moved away from the car, from the thin man. Slowly, hoping he wouldn't notice. She was afraid of him, afraid he might hurt her. She didn't know him, had never met him before. But he seemed to want something from her.

He came after her. He grabbed her arm, forcing her to look him in the face. He was probably over thirty, his face a landscape with wrinkles for rivers. Skinny as a pole. He was way old.

His face cracked and she realized he was smiling at her.

"You're hot," he said.

"Get your hands off me." She jerked away. Without waiting to see if he was following, she ran across the field toward the bluff's edge. She didn't want him near her, didn't want him to touch her.

She ran through the edge of the woods toward the Maiden Rock. It wasn't imposing at all, just looked like a bump at the edge of the field. But the drop-off the other side was about three hundred feet down. Looking up at it from Highway 35, the Maiden Rock was as tall as a skyscraper.

It had been her idea to come here. She knew this place so well. The Maiden Rock. She had climbed it many times from the highway. There was a steep path that wound up a gulley, then cut across the limestone sides of the bluff. It wasn't too hard to climb, took about a half hour to get to the top. The rock towered about twenty stories above the road and the river.

Tonight they had driven in through a farmer's land and were already on top. From here, you couldn't even tell that the field dropped off to the lake. You couldn't even see the limestone outcropping that was called Maiden Rock. She always thought of the story of Winona, the Indian maiden, when she was here.

The moon was blastingly bright and she could easily see her way. She felt powerful, with that cool night vision where everything was clear, in focus. The heart of the earth pulsed. Everything connected to her, moved through her. There was nothing she couldn't do.

When she stopped on the other side of the field, she could see the lake. Below her, it had grown into a glittering, gliding creature, alive. Its dark skin shone with as many twinkles as there were stars in the sky.

The thin man came up behind her and put his arms around her. His hands snaked down the neck of her Indian costume, but she stopped him. She needed to get away from him. He was evil. She could see it in his face. She wouldn't have minded so much if it had been Jared. She tried to wriggle away, but he kept groping her. He was trying to pull off her costume.

She gave in for a moment, then broke away and ran. Behind her, she heard him stumbling along.

She knew where she needed to go. Her feet were so fast they were on fire. The guy was still close behind her, catching up.

She scrambled up onto the limestone ledge, stood on the brink. She was at the edge of the Maiden Rock, the deep well of the forest below her, then the road and the water.

It looked so easy. Like walking through a door.

That whole other world out there.

Hitch came up behind her and tried to grab her.

As she stepped off, she heard him scream. What he didn't understand, what she had only just realized was ...

She could fly.

CHAPTER 1

1:12 a.m.

Claire woke with the full moon pouring in the bedroom window and acute anxiety flooding her body. *Meg.* The thought jolted her upright. *Where is Meg?*

Then she remembered. Her daughter was staying with Krista Jorgenson, a friend from school. Lying back, she pulled up the covers. She tried to relax her muscles one by one, but still felt uneasy.

Claire had always known that another sense comes to mothers as soon as they give birth to a child—the often prescient ability to know when that child is in danger, when something bad might be happening to them, a prick of fear in the night.

Next to her, Rich snored gently, sounding like a distant lawn mower. She knew if she nudged him he would turn and the snoring would stop, but often she found the sound reassuring. Claire craned her neck to see the luminescent face of her alarm clock. The numbers rolled. One fifteen. Too late to call the Jorgensons'. Way too early to get up. But she could tell it would be hard to get back to sleep.

Claire tried to talk herself down. It didn't help that as a deputy sheriff for the county she knew what trouble country kids could get up to. But Meg would be fine. Krista was a bright kid who

Meg had just started to hang around with. A bit frantic, but full of good energy.

Krista was a year older than Meg but their high school in the next town downriver, Pepin, Wisconsin, was so small—only 23 kids in Meg's class—that it wasn't unusual for them to make friends in another grade.

Halloween had fallen on a Friday this year. Since Meg was too old to go trick-or-treating, she had asked permission to go to a party and stay over at Krista's. Krista had just passed her driver's test. A big step forward in freedom for a kid in the country. Meg had just turned fifteen and was already bugging Rich to take her out to the farm fields and let her try driving.

After some thought, Claire had said yes, she could stay over at Krista's. She knew the Jorgensons only slightly. They lived in Pepin and seemed like a fine family. Besides farming, Mr. Jorgenson worked in Wabasha at the hardware store, and Mrs. Jorgenson was a part-time clerk for the township.

Meg had been so excited as she put on her costume that afternoon, saying she wanted to look just like Winona, the Ojibwe maiden. "My skin is too pale. Do you think I should put on some darker make-up?"

Claire watched her daughter in the mirror. Meg's hair was braided into a single plait down her back. The "costume" was an old brown shift of Claire's with a beaded necklace that she had bought up north one summer. She had dug back in her closet and come up with an old pair of moccasins. "I think you look perfect."

"Mom, you always say that."

"You always do look perfect. Nearly always."

"Not very sexy."

"Indian maidens aren't supposed to look sexy."

Meg laughed. "No, I suppose not. But they probably didn't wear bras."

Claire shot her a look.

"Don't worry, I've got a bra on."

Meg had developed into a lovely girl and her bra size was coming close to that of her mother's.

"Who's going to be at this party?" Claire asked.

"The usual."

"Remind me."

"Me and Krista. Curt and Kenny. You know, the gang from school."

Claire knew all the kids Meg had mentioned and mostly she liked them. "What about Jared?"

Meg made a face. "I don't think so. He's been pretty weird lately. He's sick a lot. I think he might have mono or something. You should see him. He looks like a scarecrow. His clothes hang on him."

"That's too bad."

Then Krista had honked the horn.

Claire grabbed her red hunting jacket and handed it to her. "You need to take a jacket."

Meg reluctantly took it and ran out the door. Hardly said goodbye. No kiss.

Lying in bed, Claire wondered how the Halloween party had been. She wondered if there was any drinking going on. She thought of what she had been doing at Meg's age at those kinds of parties. That really gave her something to worry about. She remembered getting a hickey in the closet of some party and having to wear turtlenecks for at least a week.

Finally she gave up trying to get back to sleep. Her mind was traveling too fast. She rolled out of bed and moved quietly to the bedroom door. She might as well go downstairs to read so she wouldn't disturb Rich. His day started early enough as a farmer, feeding the pheasants and take care of the other animals.

Recently she was waking up in the night so often that she left a blanket on the couch to curl up in. She was reading *The Lovely Bones,* an odd fairy tale of a book, as much about murder as Cinderella is about a relationship. But reading a few pages about the young girl getting abducted just made her more jangly.

The house was quiet. Usually an animal would cry out or an owl would call long and low, but it was still tonight. Not even a train threaded the silence along Lake Pepin. She let the book rest on her chest and closed her eyes.

***

3:05 a.m.

The phone rang and Claire was standing up before she was awake.

Meg?

She ran to the cordless sitting on the counter in the kitchen.

"Claire? I know it's late." Emily Jorgenson's voice whispered. "Are they there? Are they at your house?"

"What do you mean, are they here?" Claire asked. She could hear Rich's feet hit the floor upstairs.

"The girls."

"They're not at your place?"

"No, we've been waiting for them to come home. I gave them a midnight curfew. But they haven't shown up yet."

Claire didn't want to be hearing this. "You don't know where they are? Are they still at the party?"

"We went over to see some friends and when we got home, they weren't here. I wasn't worried because it was just a little after midnight. When they didn't show by one o'clock, I called the Lunds. They said the party was over hours ago. Everyone had gone home."

"Could their car have broken down?"

"We drove to the Lunds and back. No sign of them. I hated to call you, but I'm getting pretty worried."

Rich clomped down the stairs in an old t-shirt and a pair of long johns. He sat at the bottom of the stairs and looked at her.

"Hold on." Claire covered the speaker of the phone and filled Rich in, ending with, "Where do you think they might be?"

Rich shook his head. "Krista just got her license. They probably went for a joy ride."

"I hope." She turned back to the phone. "Could they just be out driving around?"

"I suppose. Let's give them another half hour. If they don't show, I'll call you back." When Claire agreed, Emily hung up.

Claire felt her bones stiffen. This was bad. Meg didn't do things like this. She was almost too responsible. But it was hard to say what she might do if all the other kids she was with wanted to.

She turned to Rich. "Now what?"

"Take a deep breath."

"Don't do that to me," Claire snapped. "Why did I let Meg go to this party and then stay over?"

"Because she's a big girl."

She stared at him, then let her breath out. "You're right, Rich. I don't want to be one of those mothers who's afraid for their daughters to do anything, go anyplace. I don't want to keep her locked up. But, tonight I wish she were upstairs in her own bed, safe and sound."

Rich opened his arms and she walked into them. He kissed the top of her head and said, "Me too."

***

3:30 a.m.

"That's it. She's grounded." Roger Jorgenson stood next to the kitchen window, staring out, watching for the car's headlights to break the dark. Nothing.

"Roger, maybe there's a good reason."

"No good reason for not calling."

"It would be easier for Krista to call if she had a cell phone."

"She don't need a cell phone. When I was a kid we weren't even allowed to use the phone."

Emily just rolled her eyes.

"It's that Curt kid."

"I think he's a nice boy."

"You don't know what boys that age are like."

She looked at her husband. "I did. I haven't forgotten."

What Emily hated about how over-wrought Roger could get was his emotional state didn't allow any room for her to be upset. She always had to be in control, the steady one. Inside, she was collapsing with worry over their daughter. Krista had turned into even more of a wild child since her sixteenth birthday, almost as if her hormones had cranked up a notch.

Krista was what the parenting books called a "risk taker." She loved to be thrilled, to be scared.

Emily had never been like that. She had never ridden on a motorcycle, never been on a Ferris wheel, could hardly stand to go out on a boat on the lake. She hated heights, was afraid of spiders and couldn't even pick up a worm. So she had watched in astonishment as her oldest daughter had delighted in hanging by her knees from the top bars of the jungle gym, jumped out of the hay loft onto a thin mattress, and carried a garter snake around in her Halloween candy bag one year.

Emily tried to control her fears, tried not to let her children see how afraid she was—but sometimes it leaked out of her.

"Well, she's certainly not driving the car again for a very long time." Roger thumped the kitchen table for good measure.

Emily couldn't stand it. What was he thinking? She could hear her voice had gone high and thin, but she said it anyway. "Roger, stop it. I just want her safe. I'd do anything to just have her here right now."

***

3:35 a.m.

A plume of gas hit him and Jared felt his face melting. He dropped the metal canister he was siphoning the ammonia into and put his hands to his face. All he felt was wet. His skin had turned to liquid. He couldn't see, he couldn't breath. He was dissolving.

Coughs racked his throat and his eyes cried and cried. The world spun in loops around him. Ride it out, he thought.

This had happened to him before. Damn ammonia was tricky stuff. Had to be careful. He hoped it wasn't too bad this time. He couldn't afford to go to the hospital. They would know what he had been doing. Hard to say you were fertilizing your fields at three in the morning.

Jared straightened up and walked away from the tank. He took deep breaths and tried to clear his head. Pulling his t-shirt up from his waist, he toweled off his face. His nose was running; his eyes were still watering, but he could see again. He was going to be all right.

He shouldn't have tried to do this on his own, but Hitch had to go back to the trailer to get ready. They needed to make some more *glass*. The demand was increasing every day and he needed enough for himself. His demand was going up too. It always seemed to take a little more to get him where he wanted to go.

And he never got there. It was never like the first time. Now he needed meth just to get through the day, not to go crazy. It had become like oxygen, that necessary.

Jared looked across the field to the farmhouse. No lights on. Middle of the night and everyone was sleeping. He went back to the thousand-gallon fertilizer tank and resealed the hose to his canister, then started to fill it again.

He had dropped Hitch off at the trailer to get everything ready to cook up another batch. Jared had scouted out this tank yesterday. Since he knew the area, it was his job to get the ammonia. He had to be careful about it. Somebody told him the cops could arrest him just for having ammonia in his truck—in an improper container. A five-year felony, this guy said. Five years, that was more than a quarter of his life so far.

If he was careful, he could come back and get more ammonia from this same tank. The farmer might never know.

He had to watch what he was doing. The canister was full. Exercising great care, he got the top on without too much leaking out. He hoisted it to his hip and started to walk back to his truck.

His pants were falling down as he walked. None of his clothes fit anymore. He had lost about sixty pounds in the last six months. He had played football last year at the high school, but he didn't even try out this fall. Hell, he barely went to school anymore. His mom had threatened to kick him out of the house. It didn't matter. He was hardly ever home.

He jumped into the pickup truck and headed to the trailer Hitch was renting. His skin was starting to crawl. It felt like it was peeling off his face. Someday he'd wake up and he'd be so thin, he'd just walk out of his skin.

He didn't feel like he existed anymore unless he had just gotten a hit. That seemed to be all he lived for.

Jared wondered what had happened to *Winona*. That's what she had insisted on being called tonight, saying she was some kind of Indian maiden. It had felt a little weird to leave her out there at that rock, but she had a car.

Jared had always thought she was cute. He thought of driving back and checking on her, but he really needed to get the next batch made.

CHAPTER 2

4:00 a.m.

Edwin Sandstrom had to pee. It was so hard to leave the warmth of the bed, but once he had the urge, he knew he wouldn't be able to fall back asleep until he satisfied it. His middle-of-the-night wakings were becoming more frequent. Ella was bugging him to get his prostate checked. He didn't really want to hear what the doctors might have to say. No sense in fussing around with his old equipment.

As he walked down the hallway, he calculated how much liquid he'd had to drink that evening: milk with dinner, a glass of water after, then a cup of tea with Ella before bed. Maybe he should cut back on his intake.

Then he remembered that it had been Halloween. Maybe it was the candy that did it. They had bought two bags of candy, but only three kids came trick or treating. Not like twenty years ago when a crew would show up. He had eaten quite a few of the Butterfingers, his favorite. Maybe the sugar irritated his bladder, causing him to pee. He thought it as good a theory as any.

After relieving himself, he washed his hands and stooped in close to the bathroom mirror. He wondered, as he often did, who that old man was. Going to be eighty next week. Too old. But since he had married Ella he felt a new lease on life. Maybe a prostate exam wasn't a bad idea. Ella was seven years younger than he was and he didn't intend on leaving her alone at the end of her life.

Before going back to bed, Edwin peered out the bathroom window. That old beater car was still parked out by the Maiden Rock. If he could see better, he'd probably recognize it.

That old rock lured kids to it like bees to honey, always had. When he was growing up his mother had told him the ghost of Winona haunted the rock. She said sometimes at night you could hear her sing. She warned him to stay away from the rock, especially when there was a full moon, when the maiden Winona would be looking for her Indian brave. Of course, as soon as he was big enough to climb out his bedroom window, he would go out at night and sit on the rock. To his great disappointment, he never saw any ghost, but he learned to love that hypnotic view of the river sparkling in the moonlight.

He had heard a couple of cars drive out there earlier this evening. He didn't care if the local teenagers parked out at the rock for a while, but these young lovers had been at it almost all night. He had half a mind to call the sheriff, but the house was cold and his bed was warm.

Edwin steadied himself by running his hand along the wall as he walked back down the hallway. If the car was still there when he got up in the morning, he'd call. He didn't want kids camping out there. Too dangerous. The Maiden Rock had been in his family for over a hundred years. He felt like it was his responsibility

Addison Spaulding had purchased one hundred and twenty-six acres of land that included the Maiden Rock from the Indians in 1873. Edwin's great-grandfather, Gaylord Sandstrom, had bought it seventeen years later, along with forty acres of land.

As far as Edwin knew—since Winona—no one had ever fallen or jumped from the rock. He didn't want the first accident to be on his watch.

***

4:08 a.m.

Yesterday, Meg had sworn him to secrecy when he picked her up from school. She was bursting with the news that she liked a boy and he liked her. However, she hadn't said the kid's name.

Rich hadn't wanted to promise, but she assured him that she would tell her mom in the immediate future, right after the party. He wondered if he had made a mistake. Could this late night prank have anything to do with Meg's secret? He didn't see how.

Rich decided he might as well put on some coffee. Claire had left a few minutes ago to go to the Jorgenson's, but he knew he wouldn't be able to go back to sleep. He wasn't as shaken by Meg staying out late as Claire was, but he didn't feel easy about it. Meg was one of his favorite people in the world and he certainly didn't want to think about anything happening to her.

Claire took the cell phone with her. She asked him to call her if he heard anything, although reception was spotty along the bluff.

As far as he was concerned it was about time they gave Meg a cell phone. Then incidents like this would never happen. Although kids can always come up with an excuse for not answering their cell phones when they didn't feel like it. He hated the contraptions himself; he especially hated the tall blinking towers they were constructing all along the bluffs on both sides of the river so people could communicate with each other no matter what hollow or hillside they were on.

Was he a bit of a Luddite, or just turning into a crotchety old man? He liked being someplace where no one could reach him. Wasn't that what the frontier was about? Being out on your own in the wilderness? But there was little wilderness left in this world. By the time he died there might be almost none. Morbid, middle-of-the-night thoughts.

He glanced at the kitchen clock. It was a quarter after four. This time of year, it would get light shortly after six in the morning.

Meg would show up before then, he was sure. She said she would tell her mom today about this potential boyfriend.

"He's smart. He reads. He likes to talk about books and he notices things." Meg said when she tried to explain to Rich how great this kid was.

"Sounds like a real scholar."

"You know, I think he is and that's unusual these days. I've liked him for a couple months, but I never imagined he felt the same way about me." Meg bounced in the car seat next to him.

"It's a little complicated," she explained, "Another girl's involved. I'm sure it'll all work out."

"So's this guy going to be at the party tonight?" Rich asked.

Meg beamed and nodded. Rich was happy for her. She sounded ecstatic and he remembered for a flash what that burst of young love could feel like. Euphoric. Life-changing. All consuming.

Rich wondered if Meg had decided to stay out all night with this kid, if they had driven down some deserted farm road to make out and gotten stuck. But what about Krista? Maybe the three of them had driven up to the Cities on a lark. Who knew what kids would do these days? Certainly nothing he hadn't thought of or done when he was their age.

He remembered the first time he stayed out all night. He had been seventeen. Old enough to join the army, but too young to vote or drink. His father was making coffee when Rich walked in the kitchen door. He had barely glanced at Rich. Then he said, "I'm going to Wabasha to get some feed. I'll talk to you when you wake up." Rich had wished he would have blown up at him right then. Waiting had made it harder. In the end his father hadn't even been that mad. Just gave him more chores to do.

Rich was more worried about Claire than he was about Meg. She took these escapades very hard. She saw the world as an evil, dangerous place and her daughter as its primary target. He neither believed in the safety of the home, nor feared the dangers of the larger world. He figured you took care of yourself the best you could and rolled when the punches came.

He had all the confidence in the world that Meg would make her way through the worst of it better than most. She was more than a survivor; she was an adventurer.

***

4:15 a.m.

The moon was falling into the lake as Claire took a last look at it before she turned the squad car up the bluff. She wound her way past a gravel pit, then came out into cornfields, as the sky lightened in the east. Crows dotted the fields, picking at the remains of the corn. No one else was on the road.

Claire tried to persuade herself that the girls would be at the Jorgenson's when she arrived. She would be mad and then she would laugh. Kids would be kids, she would say, waiting until Meg came home to give her a piece of her mind. She debated about whether she would take Meg home with her or let her continue the so-called sleepover. She'd play it by ear. See what they had to say for themselves.

She turned in the driveway. Only the Jorgenson's pickup truck was parked by the house. Her breath caught in her throat; her heart slammed around inside her chest. Where were they?

Claire knocked on the side door and heard a voice tell her to come in. When she stepped into the kitchen, she found Emily Jorgenson sitting at the table, pulling long pieces of wool through fabric stretched over a frame.

Emily was a thick, squat woman with startlingly blue eyes and beautiful curly hair. The few times Claire had talked to her, she had found her to be reserved, with a sense of humor running underneath, but very quiet and steady.

Emily set the work down on the floor behind her chair. "No news," she said. It was both a question and an answer.

Claire shook her head. "I haven't heard anything. Rich knows to call here if he hears from them."

Emily waved her hand up in the air, then explained. "My husband went up to bed. He has to work tomorrow." Emily looked at the clock over the kitchen sink. "In a few hours."

"Did Krista say anything to you about wanting to drive into the cities or visit someone?" As the words came out of Claire's mouth, she realized she was trying to blame Krista for what had happened. Surely her darling daughter Meg would never have done anything like this if it wasn't for the bad influence of Krista. She needed to squash those thoughts. She knew Meg was capable of thinking of a myriad of naughty tricks to pull. However, Krista had always struck her as impulsive—quick to jump onto a new idea and run with it, never happy to sit still.

Emily shook her head. "No. She was just excited to have Meg staying over. She planned on making waffles for breakfast. She's never driven into the Cities alone, or even with me. I hope that isn't what they've done." Emily jumped up and pushed a chair toward Claire. "Please sit down. Can I get you something?"

Claire sat at the table. "Thanks, I'm fine. What're you working on?"

"Oh, that's just my hooking. My mom taught me how to hook and I'm working on a new rug for Krista's room. She wanted one that was all roses." Emily pulled out the rug and showed Claire the first few pink and red roses that she had done in the middle of the piece. "It calms me down."

"I could use a hobby like that."

"It's not hard to learn. I could show you."

"Thanks, maybe I'll take you up on that. I've done quilting." Claire asked, "What exactly did the Lunds say when you called over there?"

"I talked to Mr. Lund. He didn't sound too happy about being woken up. I almost expected him to hang up on me. He said the party was over and everyone was gone. He did say some kids had come to it that hadn't been invited."

"I wonder who?" Claire latched on to that comment. "We need to talk to the other kids that were at the party. They might know something. Could you write down a list of the kids you know were there?"

Emily gave her an odd smile. "Sure, but it's too early to talk to any of them. Look at the time. They're all still sleeping."

Claire shook herself. She needed to stop being a deputy. "You're right. Come to that, we probably won't need to talk to anyone but our daughters when they finally show up."

Someone pounded on the door and startled them. The two women looked at each other, but Emily said, "It's not the kids. They wouldn't knock." She stood up and pulled open the door.

A tall, thin woman walked in, wearing a handknit Scandinavian sweater. Claire knew she had seen her before, probably at the grocery store or gas station. She had sandy blonde hair pulled back in a loose ponytail. She looked tired and worried.

"Is Curt here?" the woman asked.

"Nope, none of the kids are here. Come on in, Lynn. This is the lost mothers gathering. Somehow it makes me feel better that Curt's with the girls."

Claire introduced herself and the woman smiled and said, "Oh, you're the deputy. I've seen you around."

"Your son was at the party at Lund's?"

"Yes, and he and Krista have been hanging out together so I thought he might have come over here. I was looking for his car. When I drove up to your place, I saw the lights on in the kitchen so I decided to knock. I'm not that worried, more mad. He's stayed out late before, but never this late."

"Does he have a cell phone?"

"Yes, but he didn't take it with him. He said it wouldn't go with his costume. He was Robin Hood."

"He could have stuffed it in his quiver."

Lynn looked at Claire. "Well, since you're the cop, what should we do? Do we report them missing?"

"Not this soon. I still think they're going to show up any minute. I think it's time to go over to Lund's and see what the kids over there know."

Emily hesitated. "I hate to wake them up again. We just went over there two hours ago."

Claire was accustomed to barging in on people in the middle of the night and didn't think that much of it. When she needed information, she would go and get it. Not so with these other mothers. And, wasn't that all she was right now, simply a worried mother, not a deputy sheriff looking for a bad guy?

CHAPTER 3

5:00 a.m.

Claire managed to sit still and talk with the two women over a cup of coffee, but then she had to do something. After she called Rich to check if he had heard anything and Lynn called home to check that Curt hadn't shown up, she set off for the Lund's, leaving the two women talking at the table.

Three kids missing. Oddly, the larger number did make her more comfortable. When it was only two girls, they could have been abducted, but it seemed less likely with three of them and one a boy. And the car was gone. Chances were they were out driving around. If that was the case, Meg would be grounded for a good long while. But Claire felt more comfortable about this escapade.

Over the rolling farmland, golden light seeped out from the east, a hazy orange-pink glow. She loved how the sky painted complex and ephemeral colors hard to name in this hour before sunrise.

The Lunds lived down a road that was named after them. The county designated dead-ends for the last family that lived at the end of the road, thus *Lund Lane.* She turned down the dirt road and rolled up in front of the red-roofed farm house.

The house looked quiet. An old golden dog raised up on his front legs and gave a low, sleepy bark, then flopped back down again. Claire hated to wake up the family. She hesitated, sat in the car for a few minutes, and then saw the door of the farmhouse open. A young girl stepped out and walked toward the squad car. She was wearing a pink chenille bathrobe with rubber boots on her feet.

As she came closer, Claire recognized Sally Lund. She had grown up over the summer, gone from being a tow-headed tomboy to a lanky teen-aged girl with lovely long blonde hair. Claire was pretty sure Sally was a year younger than Meg, but she looked older and was certainly taller.

"Hi, Mrs. Watkins," Sally said as she approached the car. "What're you doing here?"

"I'm looking for Meg, Krista and Curt. You know where they went after the party?"

Sally shivered in her bathrobe. "They left when everyone did. I guess I thought they were all going home."

"Anything odd happen at the party?"

Sally cocked her head. "Not really, except at the end."

"What happened then?"

"They had a fight."

"Who? What kind of fight?"

"I'm not really sure. I think it was about Curt. I think Meg and Krista were fighting over him."

"I can hardly believe that. They were fighting over Curt?" She had a hard time imaging her daughter fighting, especially over a boy. "Hitting each other?"

"No, just arguing. But loud. I think it was over Curt. I didn't pay too much attention. It happened right as everyone was leaving. Some other guys showed up and then everyone left."

"What other guys?"

"I didn't know them. One was a lot older than us. Not in high school, that's for sure. I think they were trying to crash the party. But then it was over. My parents made everyone leave."

"You don't know where they went?"

Sally shook her head. "I didn't really watch what happened. I was tired and went back in the house."

"What're you doing up so early?"

Sally smiled. "I have to go to work. I work down at the gas station. I gotta be there by six. What're you going to do to her when you find her?"

"That's a good question."

***

5:20 a.m.

The phone hadn't rung in over an hour, the night nearly over. Amy Schroeder couldn't hear any noise coming from the jail and hoped all the inmates were asleep. She stared at the clock, because at least the hands moved. It was something to watch. She couldn't see outside from where she worked and had no idea of the weather.

She was lowest on the totem pole so she had to work the late shift on Halloween, which had been a little more exciting than usual. Friday nights tended to be busy. Someone had called in when a gang of kids toilet-papered the trees around their house in Durand, three people had been hauled in for DWIs, and there was a report of juvenile girls dancing around a vehicle parked in the street in Pepin.

All that had happened earlier. She didn't expect the phone to ring again before her shift ended.

Amy stood and stretched. Somehow she had expected her job with the sheriff's department to be more physical. When she trained in law enforcement, they had emphasized physical fitness, but she had been on the job for three months and had gained five pounds. All the guys brought in junk food—Cheetos, candy bars, sunflower seeds. Maybe she'd go for a run this morning before she went to bed.

She started to do jumping jacks. They burned off a lot of calories, which is why you could only do them for a few minutes. If anyone saw her, they would think she was crazy. She was afraid most of the men in the department already were a little leery of her. She had assumed, because they had been working with a woman for a while, that it would be easy to fit into the sheriff's department, but she had been wrong. It didn't help any that she was as small as a person could be and still serve in law enforcement.

The discrimination she felt wasn't anything she could take to the sheriff and file a complaint—it was subtle and patronizing. About once a week, one of the other deputies patted her on the head. She wanted to bite them when they did that, but she held herself in check.

However, she had snapped at Bill when he offered her a hand up over a fence last time they were on duty together. Literally she had snapped at him, teeth showing. She was afraid she had done it because of all the deputies he was her favorite, and so it hurt the most when he was patronizing. That's how she read his behavior.

Bill wasn't married and as far as she knew, he wasn't seeing anyone. He was near thirty and although a little chunky, he carried his weight well. She knew he worked out, because she saw him at the gym once in a while. He kept his blond hair military-short and she'd been tempted to run a hand across it from time to time.

Amy was afraid that the story of her snapping had made the rounds of the department. The guys had started to call her "Chihuahua." She hated the nickname and knew that the more she showed her displeasure, the more they would use it.

The other surprise was that much of the work was routine, bordering on boring. Lots of paperwork, lots of driving, lots of checking up on nothing. But it was a good income for this part of the country.

She stopped her jumping jacks and was timing her pulse when the phone rang.

Amy grabbed it, slightly out of breath. "Sheriff's department."

"Hey, Amy. It's Claire."

Why was Claire calling at this hour? She didn't usually work weekends. "What's up?"

"Have you gotten any calls concerning any teenagers tonight?"

She told Claire about the toilet-papering and the dancing around the car.

"What time did the dancing happen?"

"About ten o'clock. I sent a deputy over there, but they were gone by the time he arrived. I don't know what he would have done. Enforced curfew, I guess."

"That's all?"

"Yeah, what's the matter?"

"My daughter Meg went to a party last night and hasn't shown up yet. She was staying at a friend's house and they're both missing. And a boy."

"What do you want me to do?"

"I need you to put everyone on the lookout for a car. A bunch of kids are out joy-riding. A Ford Taurus, 1990." Claire gave her the license number. "Don't make a big deal about it, but just let the squads know. They might have gone up to the cities."

"Yeah, I suppose. Kids do that."

"Call me if you hear anything," Claire said again.

"I will. I'm not on for much longer, but I'll pass the info along."

***

5:45 a.m.

Claire drove home, not knowing what else to do with herself. The worry she had inside her felt as if it was worming its way through her guts. When she walked into the house, Rich shook his head.

She walked right past him and went upstairs. On the drive home she had decided that she was going to search Meg's room. She had never read any of Meg's emails, never listened to her phone calls, barely looked in her room. She knew mothers weren't supposed to go through their daughters' things, but she had persuaded herself that this was different. Meg had brought this on herself.

Sitting down on the edge of her daughter's neatly dressed bed, she looked at the diary on the bedside table. Claire wondered if there was anything inside that small red book that would give her a clue as to where her daughter was right now. She doubted it. Plus, she didn't believe in reading something that was that private. Things would have to get worse before she'd stoop to that.

She looked at the pile of books next to Meg's diary: *To Kill a Mockingbird, Sweetblood, The Thorn Birds,* and *Pride and Prejudice.* Her daughter had definitely moved on from Harry Potter. Meg used books like drugs, a way to get distance from a world that wasn't always what she wanted.

With every breath Claire took she waited to hear the phone ring. She thought she couldn't wait any longer, but she was forced to. She had known that at some point, Meg would do something like this—skip school, steal a candy bar, skinny-dip—but she hadn't thought it would be so soon. She thought it would happen when Meg was a senior and was ready to bust out of this small-town life.

Claire leaned over and grabbed her daugher's pillow, just wanting to hold the smell of her. Underneath, she found a folded note. Under normal circumstances, she would never have read it. If everything turned out fine, she would never tell Meg she had even seen it. But she needed to know what was going on in Meg's life right now that might make her stay out all night.

The note was on narrow-lined paper and folded as small as it could fold. Carefully Claire undid it. She held it arm's length from her eyes; she didn't have her new reading glasses handy.

U know what I want. U want what I want. B strong and clear. Thats all it takes.
U & I 4ever.

The phone rang. Rich answered it before it had a chance to sound again. Claire stood at the top of the stairs and listened.

"No, nothing. You haven't heard anything either?"

He must be talking to Emily. Claire perched on the top stairs. She could feel tears pushing to get out. She fought them back; she needed to see clearly now.

She couldn't stay in this house. She had to be out actively looking for the kids. Driving around helped her feel like she was accomplishing something, even if it was only using up gas. She would go to Meg's favorite haunts: the lake, the gravel pit, the winding road up toward Gaylord's.

Rich looked up at her as she came down the stairs. "That was Emily."

"I figured."

"She's sounding worried."

"Me, too." Claire looked at Rich. Even after three years, she couldn't always read him. "How about you?"

"I'm starting to get there. This is so unlike Meg."

"She's a teenager."

"She knows we would worry."

"She probably thinks we wouldn't even know yet," Claire pointed out, trying to sound more positive than she felt. "Maybe they thought the Jorgensons wouldn't check on them."

"That's true."

"Rich, do you know if Meg has a boyfriend?"

Rich turned away and poured himself another cup of coffee.

He knew something. This time Claire could tell. He was trying to think how to say it. She just needed the truth.

"I don't care if you know something I don't know. I just found a note upstairs and it read like a love note."

He sat back down at the table and gave her a grimace of a smile. "Meg thought she might have a boyfriend. She wasn't sure. I should have told you, but ... she said she'd know after tonight. She wanted to tell you herself."

"I think that's good. I mean, who was he? Was he a nice kid?"

"I don't know. She didn't tell me. She said he was a really nice kid."

"God, what if he wasn't a nice kid? What if he did something to her?"

CHAPTER 4

6:00 a.m.

Unlike some old fogeys his age, Edwin still drank coffee—three cups every morning. He had started when he was ten years old, when coffee was brought out to the fields for mid-morning breaks. He would drink it, he hoped, until the day he died. Every night, he set the coffee-maker for 5:45. He swore that he could smell the rich aroma in bed. It pulled him down the stairs.

This morning, he left Ella sleeping, arm wrapped around her pillow. She was such a quiet sleeper, he hardly knew she was in bed with him. Betty had snored and thrashed through the night. He pulled the covers up over Ella's shoulder and patted her. Sometimes, being in bed with her, he felt unfaithful to his first wife. Hard to get over having slept with one woman for fifty years, then sleeping with another. But he liked the slightly illicit feeling of having Ella next to him.

The stairs were his first trial of the day. He had to go down using his bad leg first. The steps were steep and narrow, tucked into a small space in the house. If he was smart he would have them enlarged, but he was accustomed to them, knew how to manage them. He always kept a tight grip on the railing.

Once in the kitchen he went to the dishwasher, opened it and got out a mug. Ella had insisted they install a dishwasher when she moved in. She had scolded him about not having put one in for his first wife. He tried to tell her that Betty had liked doing the dishes, but Ella wouldn't believe him.

She had changed a few other things, even the bedroom they slept in, and he had let her. He felt it was a kind of exorcism, even though Ella and Betty had always been good friends. Ella had to make these changes in order to claim the old farmhouse and he was glad to pay for them.

He poured himself the first cup of coffee and walked to the window. The car was still there.

Darn kids! He hated to make a fuss, but it was necessary. If he called the sheriff and the deputies came out, it would spread through the community that he had reported these kids. This news would act as a deterrent to all the other teenagers who wanted to come park on his land.

He picked up the phone and dialed the sheriff's number.

He didn't mind if people climbed up to Maiden Rock from the road, but he didn't want them driving in through his land. When they made the hike up from the road, he felt like they deserved to sit on the rock and enjoy the view. They never stayed long either, because they had to climb down the bluff and no one wanted to do that in the dark. It was too dangerous.

***

6:15 a.m.

Bridget looked in on her three-year-old daughter before she went downstairs to start the day. Rachel was stretched out on her back, her face open and calm. Just looking at her daughter made

Bridget happy. She seemed so content. Rachel, like her mother, didn't like to get up early. On weekends, she could easily sleep in until eight or nine. Bridget let her, she understood.

Her ex-husband Chuck was coming to get Rachel today. He took her once a month for an overnight, then usually one other evening a month. It wasn't as often as many divorced fathers had their children, but it was enough so that Chuck and Rachel had a real connection. Bridget didn't know if she would have liked him to have visitation more often. She did look forward to her nights off and often planned something fun to do: a movie she wouldn't have watched if Rachel was around, a trip into the Cities, a night out with her sister Claire.

But for tonight she had planned nothing. Maybe she'd call and see if Claire wanted to go into the Cities with her. Shoe shopping was always an activity they both enjoyed. Her notion of what constituted a good shoe had changed considerably since she had moved to the country, clod-hoppers were often on her feet now—good solid-soled shoes that tied tight and, if possible, were waterproof. Such shoes tended to make your feet look about two sizes larger.

Bridget slipped down the stairs quietly and walked to the back door. Since moving to this small town, her morning ritual had become stepping into the back porch and reading the thermometer. When she opened the door, she guessed it was about fifty degrees out. Fall tang was in the air. The thermometer surprised her—thirty-five degrees. They'd had a light frost already, but were due for a heavy one.

She heard an odd noise and a whoosh and looked over the backyard to the field at the bottom of the bluff.

A dark bird came sailing down out of the denseness of trees and landed in the tall grass that rimmed the bluff. Another one.

A whole bevy of turkey must have roosted up in the trees. She shivered and watched three more wild turkeys awkwardly fling themselves into the day. They were such prehistoric creatures: large, black, and lumpy. Looking at turkeys, it was easy to see the connection between dinosaurs and birds. Often, when she got ready for work, they speckled the fields, bent over eating leftover grains. They would wander across the highway and take their time as cars screeched to a halt for them.

She shivered again and hugged her bathrobe around her.

The phone rang. She stood still for a moment, wondering who it could be. She prayed it wasn't work. If it was somebody calling in sick she would say she couldn't fill in. She needed this day off. She wouldn't get another whole day to herself for over a month.

Reluctantly, she walked into the house and picked up the phone.

She was happy when it was only Rich on the other end. "Good morning, this is a little on the early side even for you."

"I have a favor to ask," he said.

She didn't like the tone of his voice; it sounded clenched. "A favor? What's going on?"

"Could you come over here and man the phone?"

"What's going on, Rich?"

***

6:16 a.m.

Jared woke with a jerk. He needed it.

Bugs, he could feel them in his mouth. His gums were crawling with bugs. He rubbed at them, but they didn't go away. Tunneling into his teeth.

Something wet on his fingers. He looked down and saw streaks of blood. He wiped them on his shirt front.

He needed to tweak bad.

Where was he?

He knew he was in his car, but he couldn't see out his car windows. When he opened the door, he saw mist swirling over the fields.

He had gone to get Hitch the ammonia.

Then he saw his Aunt Letty's trailer.

Aunt Letty was his mother's sister. She'd been a nurse at the People's clinic in Wabasha until about a few years ago, when she had been caught stealing some Oxycontin. She was put on probation, but seemed to go downhill after that. Since then, his mother didn't like him hanging around with Letty.

His mother had good reason. Letty turned him onto meth last summer. He'd been using regularly ever since. When Hitch had come to live with her, getting meth got a whole lot easier. They just cooked it up every couple days. Hitch called him his "sous-chef." Once Jared asked him what that meant. Hitch said, "Undercooked."

Jared grabbed the metal canister full of ammonia from the floor of the car and walked toward the trailer. No sense knocking. He just walked in. No one hardly ever slept here, except Davy, Letty's three-year-old son. He could sleep through anything. The little boy had learned to go into his room and sleep when he needed to.

The trailer was wall-to-wall garbage and smelled like a rank boy's locker room. Letty didn't bother to clean anymore,

Hitch just messed things up again when he made the next batch of meth.

Hitch came walking out of his aunt's bedroom. "What took you so long? You got the stuff?"

"Yeah, I got it. Man, for a second I fell asleep in the driveway."

"Let's get going. We got deliveries to make."

His aunt came up behind Hitch, tying a bathrobe around her waist. She grunted at him.

Once, Letty had been beautiful.

Jared remembered how glamorous he thought his aunt was when he was little: long dark brown hair, big blue eyes, and a smile a mile wide. She had looked like a country singer.

"Hey," he said to her.

"You got it?" she asked.

He nodded.

Now Letty looked older than his mom. Her skin was dark under her eyes, her hair was thin and greasy, and she had lost some teeth. A bad case of "meth mouth." Her clothes hung on her wire-thin body.

If he didn't know better, he would have thought she was older than his grandmother, her mother. Grandma wouldn't even talk to her anymore. She had given up on Letty, said Letty was killing herself and she didn't want no part of it.

Now, Grandma wouldn't talk to him either.

Jared wondered if he was killing himself.

He had tried once or twice to quit tweaking. He stayed clean at his mom's house for four days, curled up in bed and feeling all the skin on his body being pulled off of him at once. Every square inch of flesh hurt. Every hair follicle shrieked. His eyeballs wept. His nose ran. He couldn't stand it. The morning of the fifth day he managed to get out of bed and came straight to the trailer. That was three months ago.

Davy came wandering out of his room, his hand in his mouth, wearing a T-shirt and jeans. No one had even bothered to get him ready for bed.

Jared liked Davy. He was a good kid, not much trouble. Very quiet. Big eyes that watched everything.

Davy had come to stay with Jared's family when his mom was in prison. Now the boy was back living with Letty, but Letty was too fucked up to take good care of him. Jared tried to keep an eye on the kid, but he wasn't much use either.

"Hey, Davy, it's not time to get up," Jared grabbed him by the shoulders. The kid was so tiny. He didn't even come up to Jared's belt buckle.

Davy turned his big blue eyes up to Jared, rubbed his face, then pointed at his belly. "I'm hungry."

"Come on, buddy. I'll make you a peanut butter sandwich."

Jared dug around in the kitchen. But Hitch just yelled at him to get out of the way. He was lining up all the ingredients for the next batch of meth.

Finally, in the bottom of a drawer, Jared found some old saltine crackers. He took a handful of them and gave them to Davy. Then he pushed him back into his room and standing in the doorway, watched him climb up onto his bed. "Now you stay there. We're busy out here."

The little boy shoved the whole pile of crackers into his mouth and started sucking on them. He stared at Jared. Jared didn't have time to take care of Davy. He needed to help Hitch get the next batch ready. He needed a hit bad.

He closed the door to Davy's bedroom. Behind him he heard a crack and sizzle as Hitch fired up the stove.

"Everything all right?" he yelled.

"Get over here and help me, godammit."

He reached up and latched the lock on the door so Davy couldn't get out of his bedroom.

You never knew what might happen when they were making meth and he didn't want the little boy to get hurt.

CHAPTER 5

"Wich," the little girl held out her arms. When he reached for her, she flung herself out of Bridget's grasp, trusting that he would catch her.

Rich had been an only child and had never been around small children much. He couldn't believe how easy they were to love.

Bridget's daughter Rachel had wild, curly red hair, big blue eyes, and strawberry pink lips. She wasn't a beauty, but she was so full of life. Her eyes looked deeply into everything.

He held Rachel up high so her face was level with his. She reached out and gently touched his face.

"Wha's at?" she asked.

"I cut myself shaving."

"Oh," she said seriously. "Be berry careful." Then she held up a baby finger wrapped in a huge band-aid. "I cut myself on a fall down."

"Terrible."

"Mommy fix it."

"She's brilliant."

Bridget followed him into the house. "Any news?"

"Nothing. Not a peep. Thanks for coming over. I need to get out of here." He walked into the living room. "Where could she be? I keep going over various scenarios in my mind and it's driving me crazy."

Bridget touched his arm. "You don't think anything's really wrong, do you? Meg's such a good kid."

Rich agreed. "I know. But you know what it's like when the other kids want to do something."

"Yeah. And even good kids need to be bad."

"How old were you when you stayed out all night long?"

Bridget shook her head. "I have to confess I was a goody two shoes. I don't think I did anything wild like that until I went to college and then no one really cared."

"I don't care if she drove up to the cities. I just want her to come home safe and sound."

"She will."

Rachel listened to their conversation, then asked, "Whew's my Meg?"

Bridget answered, "She's not home."

Rich set Rachel down on the couch. She slid off and ran over to the bookshelf. They kept a pile of books for her there, some of Meg's old favorites: *Winnie the Pooh, Curious George,* and *Twinkle Toes.*

"Wead, Wich, wead!" she ordered Rich, holding out a book.

"Sorry, pumpkin. I have to go out for a while." He bent down to look her in the face. "You and your mom are going to babysit our house."

The phone rang. Rich grabbed it before the next ring. "Yeah?" he answered. It was Claire. The sheriff's department had gotten a call about a car sitting out by Maiden Rock. It sounded like it might be Krista's car.

"I'm on my way there now," Claire said and he could hear the worry in her voice.

"I'm right behind you," he said. "Bridget's here, manning the fort."

Grabbing his coat, he waved his arm in the direction of the kitchen. "Thanks for doing this, Bridget. I'll call as soon as we know anything. Help yourself to anything that's in the fridge."

"You mentioned coffee?"

He pointed at the coffeemaker on the counter. "A full pot brewing."

"Bring her home."

***

6:26 a.m.

Jared never quite knew what went wrong. It happened so fast. Hitch was in charge of the lab and Jared was only his assistant.

He went to help Hitch make the meth after he put Davy back in his room. Hitch's speciality was the "Nazi method." He claimed that this technique gave him the purest meth in the whole state. He was proud of his output.

Jared didn't know any other way of doing it. Hitch had told him that the Germans created this method during World War II. Jared didn't know if he believed him, but it was a good story. Hitch was full of stories and never quit talking.

Hitch had a direct pipeline to good ephedrine pills that came up from Mexico. Too hard to get any in the pharmacies in the states anymore. Hitch went someplace about once a week to pick up his supply of pure ephedrine. He had explained to Jared that you didn't want to use the time-release, too much crap in them to filter out.

He showed the new delivery to Jared. "Just the way I like it," he crooned. "Nothing mixed in."

Jared measured out the pills, which were tiny white dots.

"Don't get the red-coated pills," he had told Jared. "Any contaminants can jell during the baseifying. You know I got a good reputation for my product."

"Right," Jared said.

"We've got to make it fast and keep it coming because those Mexicans are moving in on our territory. You've seen. Geez, they've even got their own grocery store now in Red Wing. I don't mind them coming up here to pick our sugar beets but it rankles me to no end when they start moving in on the drug scene."

"Yeah," Jared said, watching what Hitch was doing. They had their routine down. Hitch talked and got the batch going. Jared kept track of everything.

"Don't want to bring my price down. Can hardly afford to do that. But this new crank is coming in at an awfully good price. If you see any Mexicans trying to sell at your school, you tell me. Or better yet, tell your principal. I'd bet she'd get rid of them pronto."

"Sure." Jared could feel the strain of waiting for some meth in his muscles. They would start to contract on their own. Like they were twitching for it.

Jared didn't even mind the smell anymore, stinky and foul as it was. The pungent baby-diaper smell got his juices going. His body was ready to take off again; he needed it.

He had his back to the stove and was getting ready to help Hitch strain the stuff through the filter when he heard a whooshing noise. Then an explosion rocked the trailer.

By the time he turned around, the whole pot of brew was on fire. The cabinets above the sink burst into flames. The trailer was a tinder box. The smoke smell was overpowering. He could hardly breathe. Worse than a barnyard. Urine and sulphur mixed together.

Letty was trying to get to the sink, but Jared pulled her away. Water wasn't going to stop this fire.

Hitch bolted outside.

Jared ran for the door, pulling Letty with him. Both he and Letty stumbled outside, gasping in the cool morning air. Smoke poured out the open door behind them.

His eyes were burning and his stomach was convulsing. He could hardly stand up. Then he saw Letty going back toward the trailer.

What was she thinking? The side of the trailer was burning, flames shooting through the window over the sink. But he saw her disappear inside.

Then he remembered Davy.

***

6:30 a.m.

The glow to the east was strong, a halo of light showing where the sun would rise. Low mist in the fields swirled in eddies. It would burn off quickly once the sunlight hit it.

Claire prayed that the reported car was the Jorgenson's. Driving about ten miles over the speed limit, she had to slow for the turn down the long gravel road that led to the Maiden Rock. Edwin's farm. Normally, she'd stop for a cup of coffee, but she wanted to find those kids.

Her mind seesawed back and forth. For a while, she'd be sure Meg was fine. Then she'd get mad, thinking of her daughter pulling a stunt like this. That felt good. Until she got scared all over again.

As she slalomed down the rutted dirt road, she tried not to think of what she might find: three hungover kids, a sex orgy, all three asphyxiated when they sat in the car and ran the engine, a suicide pact. She knew too much, that was her problem. She had been a cop for too long. When it came to trouble, she could see every shape or form it might take and imagine them all happening to the ones she loved.

The rusting car sat on the edge of the field, facing the bluff, away from the first gleamings of the sun. She pulled up next to it and didn't see anything move. No heads popped up at the sound of her car stopping. Good or bad, she didn't know.

Claire looked inside—empty.

She pulled open the door, which let out a loud screech. A clunker, good for nothing except driving close to home. It had been on its last legs for so long it was crawling. Inside, a couple of maps were folded and tucked into the door pockets. Cans of diet coke littered the floor in the back. No beer bottles. No cigarette butts. No condoms. That was good.

But no kids. No Meg or Krista or Curt. No sign of them. No purses, no shoes, no jackets. And that was bad.

She slid into the driver's seat and checked for the keys. First on top of the window visor. Not there. Then she snaked her hand down under the seat. At first she found nothing, but then she lifted up the mat and found two keys ringed together. She tried a key and the car started. The other key was probably to the Jorgenson's house.

Claire thought of honking the horn. It might rouse the kids if they were off in the woods, but she'd rather go in after them. She'd go out and holler, then hike down the bluff if she had to.

Leaning into the squad car, she grabbed the handset and radioed into the sheriff's department.

Amy answered, her voice sounded tired.

"You're still awake?" Claire asked, rubbing at her own eyes.

"Wilting. Long night. Another couple minutes and I can head for bed. You find the car?"

"Yeah, thanks. It's the right car. But the kids aren't here." Claire glanced over at the car. Where were they? "I'm going to go look for them. Just wanted you to know where I am."

"At the Maiden Rock, right?"

"Yeah, you come in through Sandstrom's driveway."

"Where are you going to look?"

"There's a path down the front of the bluff. I'll hike down that. They might be camping out in the woods. Maybe they're doing a Blair Witch-type deal. Who knows?"

Amy didn't say anything for a moment. "Be careful. Call back in when you know something."

"Will do."

As Claire walked toward the bluff edge, she came across a trampled-down area with a few beer cans—Budweiser, Leinenkugels. Meant nothing. Kids came up here all the time to party.

She kept walking, crossing the field, in the direction of the bluff. What had always struck her odd was that you couldn't see the Maiden Rock until you were standing right on top of it. It was visible from the highway but up on top you had no sense that right past the edge of the field and a narrow treeline was a sheer drop-off. The early morning wind blew gently at her back.

A path brought her down along the tree line. Looking through the trees, she could see the river far below. Suddenly, there it was—a limestone outcropping that looked more like a ledge, the Maiden Rock.

The sun streaked across the fields, and shadows stretched past her. She had never been up here before, but knew that teenagers were regular visitors, climbing up to the rock from the highway. Standing out on the rock, she could see Lake Pepin, a silvered blue that looked like an old cracked mirror.

Sunrise. This new light should comfort her, but it didn't. She saw the path that circled down past the rock and into the dark forest below.

Claire knew she had to step down into the darkness.

CHAPTER 6

6:35 a.m.

The path down from Maiden Rock was not well marked, only slightly larger than a deer path. Claire could barely make it out, curving down the side of the rock and then dropping into the dark of the forest.

This time of year most of the trees had lost their leaves, but the littered branches of the oaks and the dark boughs of the evergreens made it hard to see through the woods. Even though the sun was up as soon as she walked a few steps down the path, she was still in the shade of the bluff.

She stopped on the path and called out, "Meg, Krista, Curt." then listened for any rustle or response.

Nothing.

A car went by on Highway 35 far below. She could barely see it, but the lake was visible through the tree tops. She continued to walk down under the cliff and saw another path coming from the woods.

Claire decided to stay on what looked like the main path. She could explore the side trail later if she needed to. But why would the kids be down here? What could they be doing all night long? She could understand coming to the Maiden Rock on Halloween night, but couldn't think of a good reason for them to still be here unless they had fallen asleep.

Leaves lashed about above her head and she looked up. A black squirrel was running across a broad limb with a pinecone in its mouth. Storing up for winter. She stopped and listened again.

A deer bounded off far down the path. She could see the white flick of its tail. Hunting season was coming the next month and, with the rut season starting, the deer herds were spreading out over the land.

Claire called her daughter's name again, then the names of her friends. Then she let out a whistle that would carry further through the trees. Absolute silence filled the space left by her noise. Coyote and bear were seen regularly along the bluffs, but she had certainly warned off any critters in the area.

The path switchbacked gently down through the forest and when she rounded a corner she figured she was about halfway down the bluff. She'd go all the way to the road, check the wayside rest, and then make her way back up. Just to be sure. She didn't like the silence.

Scanning as far as she could into the woods on both sides of the path, she tried to see anything that looked out of place—a flash of color. Then she turned and looked back up toward the bluff. She stared up at the Maiden Rock, then let her eyes drop slowly as if they were a body falling from that great limestone ledge.

And that's when she saw the fawn-colored mound under a big oak.

At first she thought it was a deer that had been hit by a car and clambered this far up the bluff before it was felled by its injuries.

Then Claire remembered Meg's Indian costume, that same fawn color. Her heart froze. Her breath pulled deep into her body. She didn't want to go into the forest to find out what it was.

And then it was the only thing she wanted to do. Claire dove into the bushes, pushed through the low-hanging tree branches. Her pants got snagged by brambles, her feet slipped on the wet leaves. She scrambled frantically forward.

As she got closer, she could see it wasn't a deer. No matter how hard she tried to make it something else, it was clearly a person.

Claire pulled up for a second when she could make out the fringe on the Indian costume. She heard a cry as she ran foward and realized it came out of her mouth.

***

6:35 a.m.

He had left Davy locked in his room. The thought hit Jared like a landslide. The little boy was trapped in the burning trailer. The front of the trailer was burning, flames licking along the top edge like red frosting on a white cake.

If Letty had gone in after him, she wouldn't know Jared had locked the door. It wasn't an easy latch to undo. He waited to see if she'd emerge, but she didn't come out again.

He ran to the door of the trailer, shouting Letty's name. He tried to peer inside the doorway, but the smoke filled his eyes and he couldn't see. He couldn't even keep his eyes open. Coughing in the burning air, he backed up, gasping.

As Jared turned away from the trailer to catch his breath, he saw Hitch mounting his motorcycle. Jared thought of running after him, but then Hitch gunned the bike, kicking up gravel, and shot down the driveway.

Jared had to do something to help Davy, but he couldn't make himself go back into that inferno. Davy's room was on the other side of the trailer. Maybe he could get him out that way.

Jared ran around to the back of the trailer. He could tell which window was Davy's because it had a picture of an airplane stuck to it. He had given that to Davy for his birthday. The window was too high for him to reach, but there was an old wheelbarrow leaning against the trailer with a flat tire. He pushed that over to the window and stood on it. The wheelbarrow wobbled, then tipped him out.

Wedging the wheelbarrow more firmly against the side of the trailer, he climbed back into it, balancing himself. He could see into Davy's room, but couldn't see the little boy. Maybe the kid was hiding under the bed. He had done that sometimes when he was staying at Jared's house. Davy claimed it made him feel safer. Jared thought it was weird at the time. How scary does your life have to be for the shadows under the bed to be welcoming?

Jared pounded on the frame of the window, pushing inward in the middle of the glass. The pane cracked but didn't break.

Jared pounded harder. Cheap-ass construction, the window snapped in the middle, then pushed right in, coming off its track. It crashed to the floor and shattered.

A moment later, a head popped out from under the bed. Davy crawled out and stared up at Jared.

***

6:35 a.m.

Rich got out of his car. He heard a shriek coming from below the bluff line, past the Maiden Rock. He had heard such a noise come out of a rabbit carried off by a hawk—a high-pitched keening sound.

Claire's squad car was parked next to the Jorgenson's car. He recognized their old Taurus from seeing it on the road for so many years. The car was just barely held together by duct tape.

He checked both vehicles quickly, then jogged to the edge of the bluff. He knew there was a path that went down to the road, but he had never explored it. On the north side of the rock, a thick wall of brambles and gooseberries looked impenetrable. He checked the other side of the Maiden Rock and just when he was about to give up, he saw an opening, a slight break in the bushes at the edge of the clearing. As he got closer, he saw it was the beginning of a path down the bluff.

He jumped down onto the dirt path and stood still for a few moments, letting his eyes adjust to the dark. Again, he thought he heard something move below him, toward the river.

Cupping his hands around his mouth, he tilted his head back and yelled, "Claire, where are you?"

His voice sounded like a clap off the front of the limestone bluff and rolled down the hillside.

A whistle sailed up to him. He knew it was Claire. One of the skills she was most proud of, that she had learned at the police academy, was how to do a two-fingered whistle that carried miles.

He trotted down the dirt path, watching for roots and branches that might trip him up. As he came around the bottom of the limestone outcropping that was the Maiden Rock, he saw someone running up the path.

Claire charged right into him, burrowing her head into his chest, and saying, "It's not her."

"Who's not her?"

"It's not Meg. I thought it was." She lifted her face up to his and he could see she was fighting tears and losing.

"What'd you find?"

"I thought it was a deer at first. I didn't want you to see her until I told you. It's not Meg. It's Krista."

He felt the air explode out of his body and wanted to sit down, but Claire was pulling him down the path with her.

"Is she all right?"

Claire stopped, shook her dark hair, and stifled another sob. "No, she's not all right. Rich, I think she broke her neck."

"She's dead?" He couldn't believe he was asking that question.

Claire nodded. "Yes. I think she's been dead for a while. I checked her out. Nothing. No pulse, no hope. I think rigor is setting in already. Probably because of the cold."

They ran together until she pulled him off the path and he followed her through the forest. He could make out a light mound, like a pile of straw on the forest floor. And then he was standing over the girl.

Krista Jorgenson. Sixteen years old. Her head bent at an odd angle. Her hands outstretched. Long blond hair. Eyes slitted open. Not a bruise on her as far as he could tell. But there was no question that she was dead and that it had happened a while ago. Something about the silence that hovered around her said her life force was long gone.

Rich looked up. The trajectory was right. This might be where she would have landed if she jumped from the Maiden Rock. But he didn't think this is where she would have landed if she had simply fallen. It was hard to tell and he hated to think that she had jumped. However, it would explain what they were seeing.

Krista was dressed in an Indian costume that looked a lot like the one that Meg had worn.

As if she had read his mind, Claire looked at him and said, "Meg didn't tell me they both dressed like Indians."

"So where is Meg?" Rich asked.

CHAPTER 7

6:37 a.m.

Wisps of smoke were starting to leak under the edge of the door. Jared leaned over as far as he could into the room. He didn't want to climb through the window; there wasn't enough time. He needed to get the kid out of there pronto.

"Davy, come here," Jared commanded.

The little boy had crawled out from beneath the bed. He looked over at Jared and cowered.

"Davy," Jared yelled and stretched down his arms into the room, hoping to lure the boy within reach.

Davy stood still, too scared to move.

Jared had to make him move. The fire would bust through the door any second. What could he say to get him to come to him?

"Piggyback," Jared yelled. It was a game they played. "Come on, buddy, piggyback time."

Davy responded to the word and came running to him.

Jared's arms tightened around the boy. The kid was so light he hardly weighed anything. He lifted him up and out the window. Then they both fell back, off the wheelbarrow, and landed on the ground.

Jared knew they needed to get away from the trailer. He scrambled to his feet and pulled Davy with him. They ran around the side of the trailer and out into the yard, away from the heat of the blaze.

No sign of Letty. The trailer was burning brightly now, flames licked at the underside of the trees. There was no way he could go back in to the trailer to find her. She might have come out of the trailer while Jared was around the back, but he had a bad feeling about Letty.

Jared kept Davy's hand in his and walked the little boy to his car. Davy climbed into the passenger side as Jared started the car.

In the rear view mirror, he saw the whole trailer burst into flames. It blew up in one big blast, black smoke and yellow flames erupting. He hoped Letty wasn't in there. He wondered what she had run back in the trailer to get—her boy or some taste of the meth they were making.

It was time to go home. His mom would know what to do.

***

8:15 a.m.

"Easier to take her down to the road," Todd Morgan, an EMT, said to Claire. He wore a flannel shirt, jeans and a red plaid cap.

They were standing on the path about ten feet from Krista Jorgenson's body. In an earlier phone consultation, Claire and Sheriff Talbert had decided that the death should be treated as a crime. So deputies were taking photos and scouring the area for any traces of what had happened.

Claire knew the EMTs wanted to remove the body and go home. It was a Saturday. Many of them had chores to do. "It doesn't matter which way you take her. But we're not ready to let go of the body. We've still got work to do here. It might be a couple more hours."

"The ambulance is parked in the wayside rest. We'll bring up the stretcher and take her down that way."

Claire wondered if he was even listening. "Let's let Billy finish taking photos before we think of moving her."

"Mind if I smoke?"

She looked around the woods. "Don't think it's against the law to smoke outside yet."

He lit up a cigarette and carefully blew smoke away from her. "What do you think happened here?"

"Too soon to say."

"She jump?"

"I don't know. I don't want to guess." She felt like punching the nice, friendly EMT. He was musing on what might have caused the death of a teenaged girl. Claire was desperate to find her own daughter alive. She hated to think what might have happened to Krista.

But Claire had wondered too. As soon as another deputy had arrived, she had climbed back up the path and examined the Maiden Rock carefully.

The early morning sun had been full upon the rough golden limestone surface which was pockmarked with tufts of grass and dandelions. She walked over every inch of its surface, bent so that her face was close to the ground. There had been nothing to notice, not a thread, no blade of grass broken, not a scrape mark. Yet Claire was certain that Krista had been up on that rock last night and somehow had sailed off of it. She wondered if Meg had been there with her.

Meg. She could hardly stand to think about her daughter. She was staying with Krista's body until the Chief Deputy Sheriff showed up, and then she was going to join in the hunt for her daughter and Curt Olsen. Rich had gone off with two deputies to scout the woods close by the Maiden Rock. Two other deputies were up top on the bluff, going door to door, talking to farmers, searching their fields and farm roads.

Claire felt tied to her useless vigil over Krista, guarding her when she was already gone.

Up the path she saw Chief Deputy Sheriff Steward Swanson cautiously descending. He walked lightly for all the weight he was carrying, but his mouth was open and he was breathing heavily. His color was poor, had been for some time. Last thing she needed was him to get in trouble out in the woods.

"Claire," he nodded, glancing toward the crime scene. The photographer was finishing up his photos and two deputies were going over the scene.

"Stewy," she responded.

He looked right at her. "Terrible thing."

"Yes."

"Your girl?"

"We don't know where she is yet."

He shook his head and lowered his eyes. "How can we protect these kids?"

"I guess, we can't always."

"Nope, I guess not. What'd you think happened here?"

"I'm not ready to guess."

Stewy looked back up the path, then higher to the Maiden Rock. "You know in the poem the Indian maiden lands in the river."

"The poem?"

"The poem about Winona jumping from the rock. We learned it in school when we were kids. We had to memorize it. But I always wondered about that—how could she land in the river? It never made sense. I knew the river was too far away unless she could fly."

Claire had to cut short his school reverie. "I need to go tell the family."

"Really?" Stewy stepped closer to Claire. "Are you sure you want to do it?"

"I feel like I should do it." Claire held back tears. There was no way she was going to cry in front of the Deputy Sheriff.

"It's not your job. But you certainly can take it on. No one better."

"Thanks, sir."

Again he nodded toward the crime scene. "You finding anything here?"

"Nothing by the body, nothing up top. It's like she fell out of the sky."

***

8:20 a.m.

The first thing Meg saw when she opened her eyes was an eye looking back at her. Then she smelled him. His own scent of bark and salt. She had come to know it well and thought she would be able to recognize it anywhere.

She sat up in the car and pushed back her hair. "What're you doing?"

Curt laughed. "Just watching you sleep."

"Interesting?"

"Fascinating."

"I do it every night. I'm really good at it."

"Tell me more."

Then his face got closer and he kissed her gently on the lips. She felt sore there. Sore from kissing. She didn't know you could overuse those muscles. But they had done a lot of kissing last night.

"What time is it?"

"The sun's up."

She looked at her watch and was shocked. "I need to get to the Jorgenson's. I don't think Krista will be up yet, but I don't want them to worry."

"How're you going to get into the house without her parents seeing you?"

"There's a secret way. Krista showed me. You can lift the screen off her window and climb in."

"Do you think she'll still be mad?"

Meg had no doubt. "Oh, yeah. But I'd rather face her wrath now and have her get it out of her system."

Curt started the car. "Are you sure this is what you want to do? I could drive you home."

"No, I want to talk to her before any more time passes. It's better to face the hard stuff as soon as possible."

She watched him. She felt like she could watch him all day long and never get bored. His dark hair hung around his face. He had soft splotches of freckles on his nose and his eyes were rimmed with ridiculously long lashes. She even liked the small pimple he had near his nose, like an errant beauty mark.

Curt touched her hand. "I'm glad we did this."

She knew what he meant by *this*. That they declared themselves, that they told Krista last night that they liked each other. Krista had taken it harder than Meg had thought she would. Meg wouldn't have even thought of liking Curt except Krista had sounded like she was getting bored with him.

But at the party, when they finally told her, Krista had yelled and created a scene, just when everyone was leaving. Then she jumped in her car and roared off, leaving Meg stranded. But at least they had done it. The hard part was over. Now she just had to persuade Krista they could still be friends.

After the party, Curt had offered to drive her home, then somehow they found their way over to a farm road not far from his house and sat in the warmth of the car, turning the heater on when they needed it, and talked.

They talked about everything: their favorite music, their favorite books, even their favorite food—he loved beets, she hated them. She told him how she wanted to be a veterinarian. He confessed that he hoped to be a philosopher or a rock star. He couldn't sing and didn't know how to play guitar so, at the moment, he was leaning toward philosophy.

"How do philosophers earn money?" she asked him.

"I dunno. Maybe by writing books about what they think, about how they see the world. I'm not sure. Maybe they just end up teaching, but that wouldn't be so bad. I just like thinking about everything: why we're here, where we're going, what it all means. The things no one talks about in school."

"Are you an optimist or a pessimist?" she asked.

"At the moment, optimist." He looked at her and smiled. "Usually somewhere in between."

After talking for about three hours, there had been a long silence. Then Curt had leaned close and kissed her.

They hadn't said much for a while, trying to find all the ways their mouths could come together, a puzzle they turned this way and that to find the best fit. Other than gently touching her breasts through her shirt, he hadn't tried anything else. She was glad he hadn't; she wasn't sure she could have resisted him. With him, her body seemed to have a mind of its own.

Toward morning Meg had curled up in his arms and fallen asleep. She thought he had slept too.

"Did you sleep?"

"Not much. Too busy thinking."

"That's your job, philosopher," she teased him, then turned serious. "Are you going to get in trouble?"

"What? You mean about staying out all night long? Naw."

"Your parents don't care."

"Not really. They're too busy to care. They've probably both already gone to work and might not even realize I didn't come home. They'd notice the car was gone. I think they figure I'm incorrigible." Then he laughed.

That was one of the things Meg loved about him—his laugh. It was a deep laugh that pulled her into the joke. She could hardly hear it without breaking out laughing herself. Intoxicating. She realized she felt hungover though she had only drunk half a beer at the party.

Meg laughed as he started the car. "You're lucky. My mom would kill me if she knew."

CHAPTER 8

8:32 a.m.

When Claire and Rich stepped into the Jorgensons' kitchen, Roger Jorgenson was hunched over the newspaper at the large wooden table with a cup of coffee in his hand and the remnants of scrambled eggs in front of him. Emily Jorgenson was standing at the sink, putting dishes in the open dishwasher. She turned slowly to face them when they walked in the door.

Emily knew immediately. Claire could read it on her face, the way her eyes dropped, then filled, the way her mouth quivered, the way she wiped her hands as if to rid them of some horrible grime.

Roger might have known, but was not allowing it in. He scrunched the paper down and looked angry at the intrusion, mad that his daughter's misbehavior was continuing to ruin his day.

"I need to get to work," he barked.

"I'm so sorry to have to tell you ..." Claire started, but her words were arrested by a low intake of breath, close to a growl coming from Roger. Emily bent over the sink so precipitously it looked like she was trying to throw herself into the dishwater.

Roger stood. The newspaper fell out of his hands, drifting to the floor like a faint shadow, what the world had been before.

Claire began again. "Bad news …"

Claire felt Rich's arm on her waist. "I'm so sorry, but Krista has been found …" She was having trouble getting the words out. But they had to hear it, the quicker the better. "Krista's dead. We found her below the Maiden Rock."

Roger asked, "The Maiden Rock?" Something safe to focus on, puzzle over, the site of the accident.

"My baby," Emily collapsed, holding her stomach, leaning into the cabinet doors beneath the sink. "Not my baby. Oh, God, why?"

"What happened?" Roger was still standing by the table, making no move to go to his wife. He asked the question gruffly as if he needed something concrete to understand, to grasp.

"We're not sure yet. It isn't clear. Somehow she fell. It looks like she broke her neck. It would have been instantaneous. No pain." Although Claire wasn't sure about all this, she hoped it would comfort them. How could anyone tell how quickly death came? But Krista looked like she hadn't moved after her fall.

"Somehow? What do you mean?" His voice rose and he turned to look at Claire and Rich.

"We're not sure how it happened. We might never know."

"That's impossible. You tell us our daughter's dead and we might never know how she died." His voice was filled with rage.

Rich stepped in front of Claire. He said, "Roger. We're so sorry."

"You're sorry. Hell. What do you know? What do you know?" Roger slammed his chair into the table and then stomped out of the room.

Emily whimpered.

Claire bent and pulled the crying woman into her body, wrapping her arms around her. Emily needed someone to hold onto, it was clear she was drowning. Sobs clenched her body and she gave in to them.

After some time, her crying weakened and she looked up at Claire. "What do I do now?"

Claire knew she needed to pull her back into the world. Give her a task, something to do. "Let's sit at the table." She helped Emily up.

The woman shook herself like she was shedding an old skin and ran her hands down her shirt. "Would you like some coffee?"

Rich spoke up. "I'll get it. You sit down."

Rich pulled two mugs out of a cupboard—one from the Bank of Alma, the other from the Farmer's Cooperative—and filled them up with dark coffee. He handed one to Claire and sat at the table with the two women.

"I can't believe this." Emily stared at the middle of the table, at nothing.

"I know," Claire murmured, letting the woman talk.

"She was such a good kid. Happy, trying everything. How can all that be gone?" Emily looked up at them.

"Not all," Claire said, knowing Emily had to feel the deepness of her loss, but wanting to say something positive. "In some way she will always be with you."

"But I want her." Emily hit the table with her fist as her face collapsed, but she kept looking at them.

"Yes, I know." Claire said.

This statement rocked Emily. She roused. "What about your daughter? Have you found Meg?"

Claire shook her head. "Not yet. I'm going right out to look. I wanted to come and tell you the news first. Search parties are combing the area around the Maiden Rock as we speak."

"Oh, God. What happened? What were those kids doing? Why were they hanging out at the Maiden Rock?"

"I know this is hard, Emily, but I need to ask you a few questions about Krista. It might help us understand what has happened. Was she having any problems lately? You notice any change in her behavior?"

Emily looked confused. "Like what? School? Here at home? She was doing fine. Nothing was wrong. She's always been kind of keyed up. That hasn't changed."

"Was she ever depressed? Get really down about something?"

"Once in a while, around her period, she'd have a crying jag, but the next day she'd be over it. No, she was happy. I don't think she had anything going on. I would know, wouldn't I?"

"I'd think so."

Emily's head jerked. "What are you saying? Do you think she jumped? Do you think she tried to kill herself?"

Claire didn't want Emily to go any further with that thought until they had more evidence. "No, I'm not suggesting anything like that. It's just ... we're trying to see what might have happened. Could I take a look at her room? Would that be okay?"

The need to get out and look for her own daughter was overwhelming. But Claire wanted to quickly check Krista's room before anyone else got a chance to touch it. Families had been known to withhold information about suicide notes. Under twenty percent of suicides left a note, but they were always worth looking for. She knew cases where a note cleared up deaths that might otherwise have been thought murders.

A suicide note, or evidence of drug use were what she would be looking for. A quick sweep. She had to get back to Maiden Rock and look for Meg.

"Of course." Emily stood and wiped down her shirt again, her hands needed to keep busy. "I don't know how clean her room is. You know how kids are. I try to keep on her about her room …" Her voice trailed off.

"Just show me the way." Claire followed her out of the kitchen, leaving Rich at the table.

Claire walked behind Emily through the dining room, then up very steep stairs. The farmhouse was old, probably built in the twenties. The stairs had been crammed in, like an afterthought.

"You have to walk through Tammy's room. Then Krista's room is off of that," Emily explained. They walked through a sunny room that had ballerinas on the walls, and plastic horses lined up on top of a long bookshelf. "She's at a friend's. Oh, how will I tell her her sister is dead?" Emily sank down on Tammy's bed and started sobbing. Through her tears, she waved a hand at the bedroom door.

Claire gently pushed open the door to Krista's room. The one window in the small room faced east, a splash of sunlight played on the wall above the headboard of the bed. The cover on the twin bed had been pulled up but not straightened. Three pillows were mounded together. A small CD player sat next to the bed with a huge pile of CDs and earphones dangling off the bedside table.

Claire scanned the room quickly. Nothing jumped out at her. No note sitting on the pillows, on the desk, propped up on the bookshelf, easy to find. Suicide notes didn't tend to be hidden.

A pile of photos was displayed at the end of the bed. Claire picked one up from the bed. Krista. Tip dyed blonde hair that spiked out around her face and behind her ears. She looked so alive.

As she looked down at the pile of school photos, her eyes easily picked out the picture of Meg. She lifted it up automatically. Dark hair pulled back in a loose ponytail, a hint of lipstick. Looking so grown-up. Where was her darling daughter now?

Claire strode into the other room and knelt down in front of Emily. She took her shoulders in her hands and waited until the woman looked at her. "Emily, I'm so sorry. I can't tell you how sorry. I'll come back and look some other time."

Claire suddenly couldn't wait another minute to go look for her own daughter.

***

8:42 a.m.

Even though her shift was over, Amy had decided to drive by the fire that had been reported just as she was leaving. It was on her way home. She knew the woman who owned it. Letty. Amy had babysat her nephew Jared when he was little.

As she drove up to the fire, she was happy to see the volunteers were already there, spraying the fire with foam. The trailer looked like a total loss. The smell was of burned plastic and torched wood. A horrible combination. She wondered if the fumes that were billowing out from the trailer were toxic.

She got out of her car and watched the four volunteers work the rig. She recognized John Dixon. He gave her a nod when he saw her, but didn't stop working.

Trailers were the worst for fires. Amy doubted they ever saved one. It was like lighting a bag full of gas fumes. Everything was flammable.

At least, it didn't look like anyone had been there. No cars were parked right in front of the trailer. But when she walked around the side of the fire rig, she saw a small car tucked into the weeds. An old Pontiac, it looked like. She walked up to it and tried the door. When it opened, she stuck her head inside.

She noticed two things that made her stop breathing: a set of keys on the driver's seat and a kid's carseat in the back. Letty and her son. Amy hated to think where they might be.

***

8:45 a.m.

After one last kiss, Curt dropped Meg at the end of the Jorgensons' driveway. Meg started down the rutted road. She couldn't believe what she had done: stayed out all night with a boy, making out. If she pulled this little escapade off, it would be great. But what if she got caught? There'd be hell to pay.

The Jorgensons wouldn't probably get that mad if they caught her sneaking back into their house, but she was sure they would feel obligated to tell her mother. Then she'd be in big trouble.

Her mom. Meg didn't even want to go there. It wasn't that her mom would punish her so terribly—worse, she'd probably pull one of those you've-really-let-me-down strategies.

To avoid worrying about her mom, Meg went back over the events of last night. Thinking about Curt made her feel like she was swimming in really deep water—exciting and scary at the same time.

She couldn't believe it. She had a real boyfriend, one who would stay up all night and talk to her about all the things in the world. She had dreamed about finding someone like that, but wasn't sure it would happen to her until she went to college. She had always figured herself a late bloomer.

As Meg walked up the driveway, she enumerated what she liked about Curt: 1. he read books, 2. he liked Bob Dylan and the Cranberries, 3. he thought the space between her front teeth was cute, 4. he didn't believe in war, 5. he was a great kisser, 6. he wanted to stay living in the country, 7. he wanted to travel, 8. he thought Mr. Langsfeld, their science teacher, was stupid and mean, 9. he hated that animals were becoming extinct, 10. he loved to talk. What more could she want in a guy?

When she lifted her head up and looked down the driveway, she saw a line-up of cars, but didn't see Krista's car. Maybe she had parked it behind the barn.

What kind of reception would she get from Krista? Just the day before the party, Krista had been telling her that she wasn't sure she even wanted to see Curt anymore. Meg wasn't sure it would help to remind her of that. She'd have to play it by ear.

What if Krista wouldn't let her in the house? If Krista was at all mean, Meg had decided she would just leave, she would walk home. She wasn't going to argue with Krista. She would tell her mom they had a fight. But she wanted to give Krista a chance to be her old self.

Maybe she and Curt hadn't done it right last night. They had tried to tell Krista earlier, but they hadn't really had a chance until the end of the party. They had decided to do it together, so neither of them would have to bear the brunt alone. They talked it over, decided that Krista would get angry, blow up, and then quickly get over it. That's the way she was. She never focused on any one thing for long. She bounced from one idea to another with such energy.

Meg hoped she could work it out with Krista. In a short time, she had become such a good friend.

She froze as she heard voices and then saw people coming out of the Jorgensons' house. She was too far away to see who it was, but she didn't want to take a chance. She ducked into the weeds and watched.

They got into a car. As it turned, she saw that it was a squad car. Why would a squad car be there?

Shit, what if they had called the sheriff on her? Her mom?

***

8:47 a.m.

Claire was glad Rich insisted on driving. It was against sheriff's regulations for a civilian to drive a squad car, but she knew she shouldn't be behind the wheel at the moment. It was always hard delivering bad news, but when you might be the recipient yourself of the same news, it was ghastly.

Rich started the car and then jumped when the radio crackled.

Claire took the call. Just Stewy reporting they were taking the body out. He'd check in again. Six deputies were out looking for Meg and Curt.

Rich whipped around in the driveway and headed down the long rutted road. When they were halfway down it, Claire caught something move out of the corner of her eye—a flash of red. What could be that color? Too big for a cardinal.

She remembered the red hunting jacket.

"Stop!" she yelled at Rich.

Before he even had a chance to comply, she unbuckled her seat belt, opened the door, and jumped out. She fell to her knees, but pushed up and jumped down into the ditch.

Scrub trees growing on the sides of the driveway served as cover but Claire shoved through them and saw a flash of red ducking behind a cedar. She clawed her way through the remaining branches and tall grass.

She ran around the cedar and saw the red jacket ducking under a pine tree.

"Meg!" she yelled as she spurted forward. She tackled her daughter wearing the hunting jacket she had put on the night before, as she was leaving for the party. They both fell to the ground, but Claire kept a tight grip on her daughter.

Meg sat up and Claire pulled her to her chest.

"Meg, thank god. Oh, I don't know what I would have done ..." Claire started sobbing. All the tears she had held back all night came ripping out of her. She couldn't let go of Meg. The tears, a river.

"Mom, what're you doing?"

Meg tried to pull away, but Claire held her tight.

***

8:48 a.m.

Meg knew, from the moment that her mom jumped her in the bushes at the Jorgensons' driveway, that something was horridly wrong, even before her mom started sobbing.

But her mother's tears convinced her it was very, very bad. She had never heard her mother cry like that before, even when her father died. It sounded like she was crying up her guts.

She had to help her mother out of the ditch alongside the driveway, holding her so she didn't fall. Her mother wouldn't stop holding onto her and sobbing. Rich stood at the edge of the driveway and helped them onto the gravel.

Meg looked at Rich and asked, "Who died?"

CHAPTER 9

November 3, 8 a.m.

Meg stood at the bottom of her driveway and Highway 35, waiting for the school bus. She had a hard time believing that school would happen, that life would go on as if nothing had happened. She had a hard time.

That morning her mother had told her she didn't have to go to school. Even Rich had suggested that she stay home, but she didn't want to put off the inevitable. They didn't understand. It would only get harder to see all her friends at school if she waited. All Krista's friends.

Especially Curt. He had called several times over the weekend, but once she had pretended she was sleeping, and the other time she had flat out refused to come to the phone. He got the message and didn't call again. But he deserved to hear straight from her what she was feeling.

Meg had a pile of Kleenex stuffed in the pocket of her hooded sweatshirt. Even thinking about the fact that she wouldn't be sitting next to Krista in third hour made her cry.

As she waited, questions kept buzzing around inside her head. Why had she decided to tell Krista about Curt at the party? How stupid was that? She should have waited until they were at Krista's house where she could have explained it all to her and then handled her anger face to face. Instead, she had chickened out. Curt and she had told Krista at the party, thinking that way she wouldn't make a scene. Because of this stupid decision, Krista was dead.

Blinking her eyes to clear them, Meg saw the school bus coming down the highway. She wasn't looking forward to the ride. She wasn't looking forward to anything she had to do today, or the rest of her life.

The bus stopped and the door swung open. Mr. Jensen had his hat turned backwards as usual, and said, "Good morning," like he always did. Then he added, "Sorry to hear about your friend."

"Thanks," Meg mumbled and slunk halfway down the bus aisle. She didn't want anyone to sit with her so she put her books next to her on the seat. She stared out the window and tried to see the fields as they drove by. But it was like she was blind. She couldn't see the world anymore. Just what she was feeling.

This year in world literature she had read a French poem in which the gray sky was described as being like the cover of a pot. That's how she felt. Like she was inside a container and someone had closed down her whole world.

Her mother had told her she couldn't go anywhere unnecessary for a month. In other words, she was grounded, but the weird thing about it was that Meg felt like it wasn't just a punishment, but rather a way for her mom to feel safe. For one whole month she wouldn't have to worry about where Meg was.

Meg didn't really care anyway. There was no place to go, nothing she wanted to see or do. Life, which two days ago had seemed like it could get no better, was suddenly hardly worth living.

One of the Swenson twins looked like she wanted to sit with Meg, but Meg ignored her and she walked farther down the aisle.

As always, when Meg got off the bus at school, Curt was waiting for her. Curt had always been waiting for them—Krista and her—every morning. He bent his head down toward her and smiled. Meg felt her heart turn in her chest.

"Hey," he said, walking up to her.

Meg felt like she was seeing him for the first time. His tall, skinny body towered over her. He couldn't afford to lose any weight. She felt protective of him for a moment, then pushed that feeling away.

"I called you a couple times. I really wanted to talk to you," he said. "How're you doing?"

Meg had rehearsed her speech. "I don't want to talk. I don't have any words for this."

"Meg, that's a little melo," he said gently.

That word took her by surprise. It was in their language. "Melo" was short for melodramatic. A secret word they had created together.

This wasn't going to work.

She tried to walk past him, but he grabbed her arm. "Meg, I didn't mean that. I'm feeling really bad too. But we have to help each other. We have to talk it out. Krista was my friend longer than she was yours."

How could he even try to quantify a friendship like that—by who knew her the longest? Meg wanted to scream at him. But she wouldn't. It wasn't the right place, it would never be the right time.

She felt someone grab her arm, then pull on her. When Meg looked down, she was staring at Krista's little sister Tammy, who was three years younger than her. Tammy's eyes were red and swollen from crying, but her mouth was mad. "I want to know what happened to my sister."

"Tammy." Meg tried to put an arm around Tammy. She didn't know her well, but they had always been friendly. Her heart hurt for how Tammy must be feeling.

Tammy pushed Meg's arm away. "What did you do?" she screamed. "You were supposed to be her friend. How could you let her go with those other people?" Then she turned on Curt. "Big boyfriend you are. Where were you when my sister died?"

Curt started to say something, but Tammy cut him off. "I heard what happened. You two left together. If it wasn't for you, my sister would still be alive. I hate you. I hate both of you."

She ran off before they could say anything. Meg felt another weight drop on her shoulders and her stomach turned. She felt sick all over.

"I can't do this," Meg said.

"I know. I don't want to believe she's dead either." Curt nodded.

"I just think it's over."

"What do you mean?"

She looked him straight in the face and said, "Tammy's right. We are responsible for Krista's death. We killed her. We should have waited to tell her—not done it at the party."

Curt stared at her. His face grew still. His eyes widened. "I see what you mean. It is our fault, isn't it?"

She nodded. She knew he would understand. That's what she loved about him.

"Why does everything have to go bad like this?" he asked and reluctantly let go of her arm.

She had no answer. She didn't know why things worked out the way they did.

When she walked away, he didn't try to stop her.

That was it. The love of her life so far was over.

Meg walked into school by herself. Tonya Holbrook walked up and said how horrible it was about Krista. Meg took out a Kleenex and pressed it to her eyes. These tears, she knew, were for herself.

***

8:30 a.m.

Arlene stood in the hallway and quietly pushed open the door to her son's room. Jared mumbled and stirred but didn't wake. His long dark hair haloed his head.

In sleep her son looked like an angel. Always had. But she knew that the sleep he had finally dropped into was as deep as death. She had tried to wake him twice already this morning and he wouldn't rouse. She leaned in closer to make sure he was still breathing.

When Jared had brought Davy home two days ago, she could tell that he was strung out on that drug again. When she accused him, he didn't say he wasn't. But he promised—this time he really promised her—he would go straight.

He didn't sleep at all the first night he was back, watching TV and smoking cigarette after cigarette, picking at scabs on his hands. Then he crashed about four o'clock yesterday afternoon. That was twenty hours ago. Arlene hoped he would wake up sometime today. But what she really hoped was that he could stop taking that awful drug, that meth.

But hope felt like sand, nothing you could grab onto. As her mom used to say, *wish in one hand and spit in the other and see which one gets full first.* Arlene had fed Davy and set him down in front of the TV. Her heart broke to see how skinny that little boy was.

What was the matter with her sister?

The matter might be that she was dead.

Jared had told Arlene about the fire, said he wasn't sure what had happened to Letty. Then Amy had called. Odd that Jared's former babysitter was now a deputy sheriff.

Arlene had always liked Amy, thought she would do something with herself even as a kid. Amy had said how sorry she was about Letty's trailer burning down. Then she asked her a bunch of questions, said it was too early to tell if there was a body in the trailer. The fire had burned hot and they were still sifting through the debris.

Arlene didn't mention that she already knew about the fire, that Jared had been there. No sense involving him in that mess. Arlene was glad she could tell Amy that they had Davy, and that he was fine.

Arlene half wished her sister was dead. It would be a blessing to know Letty was finally released from this horrible life she had fallen into. Davy didn't deserve to live like that. Arlene had tried to keep Davy the last time he had stayed with her, but Letty wouldn't hear of it.

This time, if Letty was still alive, Arlene would insist on keeping Davy, unless Letty cleaned up. Arlene was determined not to let the little boy go back to that hellish existence.

A tinny blast of music came from a pile of clothes on the floor—Jared's cell phone ringing. Arlene scrambled to find it before Jared woke up. There was only one person who would call him on that phone and she meant to put an end to it. She found the phone in the pocket of a pair of dirty jeans and ran out of the room with it.

For a moment she thought of answering it, but she didn't want to talk to that evil man. She had seen him once when he had stopped by the house. Jared hadn't invited him in and she never learned who he was, but she knew what he was to Jared. His dealer. With a shrunken face and steely eyes, she thought he looked like Satan reincarnate. And Arlene didn't really believe in the Devil.

She turned the phone off and stood in the kitchen, looking out the back window. She checked on Davy, who was still sitting happily in front of the TV, swaddled in a bundle of blankets with a bowl of Cheerios. Carefully he would lift one round circle of cereal up and put it in his mouth.

Arlene slipped away from him, then opened the back door and stepped outside. The air was raw, not quite freezing but threatening rain. She walked out back toward the pond. Soon the water would freeze over.

Standing in the rushes by the edge of the pond, she threw that damn phone as far as she could into the murky water. Its entry made a satisfying plop and she watched it sink.

Once back in the house, Arlene wiped down the counters of the kitchen. She couldn't leave the house as long as Jared was still sleeping. For that matter, she couldn't leave it when he woke up. She didn't trust him alone.

When the wall phone rang, she jumped, then regained her composure and answered it.

She recognized Amy's voice again, this time telling her that a body had been discovered in the rubble of the trailer. Probably a woman. All her clothes burned off. Pretty unrecognizable. Amy asked her the name of her sister's dentist.

Arlene leaned over the kitchen counter and almost started to laugh. "She doesn't have a dentist. She hardly has any teeth left. God, Amy, she was a meth addict."

There was silence on the other end of the line. Then the woman said, "Yeah, I see. This information might help us."

"I'm sure it's my sister," Arlene said.

"We'll check into it."

"I'm sure."

"I'm sorry."

"You don't need to be sorry," Arlene said, then realized she was being churlish. "I mean, thanks, but she wasn't having much of a life lately."

Arlene sat down on the living room floor next to Davy and watched Teletubbies. She found the slow movements of the colorful round creatures very soothing, the childish voices calming. Sometimes she turned the show on when she was home all alone and didn't know where Jared was.

She looked up at the family portrait that had been taken five years ago. They had been four: her husband Jeff, Jared and Julie. A perfect family—the right number of kids, a boy and a girl. They all got along. Jeff died the next summer. Collapsed of an aneurysm. Julie went off to college in New York, far away. Arlene missed her constantly, she was such a good kid. Just her and Jared left. And now Davy. She was glad Jeff hadn't been alive to see what was happening to Jared. But maybe if he were still alive Jared wouldn't have started doping.

Maybe this time she could help Jared.

She pulled Davy into her lap, his soft sweet body giving her comfort, and watched plump gentle creatures bounce around an imaginary landscape.

***

2 p.m.

After reading the same paragraph over three times, Claire realized she couldn't focus on her work. All she could think about was Meg and how she was not handling this crisis. Her daughter was in a difficult time of life anyway—the early teenage years—when it feels like your skin has been pulled off your body. Very vulnerable. And now her best friend had jumped off a cliff.

What it boiled down to was that her daughter was blaming herself for her friend's death and there was nothing Claire could do about it.

Meg would hardly talk to her. As far as Claire knew, she would hardly talk period. All Meg had done, the whole weekend, was curl up in bed and pretend she was sleeping. She had even refused to talk to her friend Curt when he had called.

Claire was jarred out of her thoughts when the phone on her desk rang. She picked it up before it rang again and said her name.

Without any hello, the male voice on the phone stated, "Got the results on the toxicology report on that young girl—Krista Jorgenson."

The call surprised Claire. She had almost forgotten that they routinely run those tests on accidental deaths and that she had requested they call her with the results.

Claire grabbed a post-it note. "Okay. Shoot."

"Alcohol level .05. Methamphetamine came in at .04 milligrams per liter of blood."

Claire's hand wrote .05. Then it stopped. "What?"

"She had some meth in her."

"Are you sure?" Claire stood up and almost pulled the phone off her desk. "I can't believe that."

"Did you know her?"

"Yeah. Pretty well."

Claire remembered Krista dancing in the kitchen. Meg and she had come over to the house to make chocolate chip cookies. They had put on some music and were dancing around the kitchen, eating the dough while the cookies baked. It seemed to Claire that Krista had never stopped moving. Why would she need to use methamphetamines with that kind of energy?

"How much is that? .04?"

"A healthy dose."

"Probably her first time," Claire said, defending Krista.

"Then it would have hit her pretty hard."

"Yeah, I guess so." Claire was standing. "Can you fax me this info?"

"You got it."

As Claire left the sheriff's department, she told the secretary she would be gone the rest of the afternoon. She jumped in her squad car and headed west on 25, then south on 35. She pulled up to the high school before two o'clock. Meg would still be in her last hour class.

Claire walked into the main office and asked that they pull her daughter out of class. The secretary called down to the room without asking why. Claire stepped out into the hallway to meet her.

She saw her daughter coming toward her with her lime-green backpack hanging off one shoulder and her feet dragging.

Meg stopped in front of her. She looked tired and anxious. "Mom, what are you doing here?"

"You want to go outside?"

"No."

"I have to tell you something."

Meg's face started to twist. "Not anything bad?"

"Let's step outside."

"Mom," Meg pleaded.

Claire took her daughter by the arm, led her gently out the school door, then into the squad car.

Once they were seated Claire said, "Krista's death had nothing to do with you. It's starting to look like it might not exactly have been a suicide. I got the toxicology report back on Krista. She had an alcohol level of .05."

"So. She had a couple beers."

"There's more. The bloodwork showed that she had methamphetamine in her system."

"What?"

"Meth."

"I know, Mom. I know what it is. But no way. Not Krista. She never did any drugs. Ever. And I would know."

Claire asked, "How would you know for sure?"

"Because we talked about it. Sure, she drank a beer or two. What kid around here doesn't? But she didn't even like any other alcohol and she had never tried any other kind of drug. Just like me. She told me that."

"Okay. I believe you. But she did have it in her system. Something happened to make her take it."

"Why would she do that?" Meg asked, then slammed her backpack to the floor of the car. "Fuck."

Claire couldn't stop herself. "Meg."

"Double fuck." Meg kicked her backpack with her foot. "I can't believe this. Where did she get it?"

"I thought maybe you could tell me."

"How would I know? Not at the party. As far as I know no one had any meth there."

"Was there anyone there you didn't know?"

Meg sat still for a moment. "I think a car drove up as we were leaving. I'm not sure. I was upset by Krista's reaction to what I had just told her."

"Maybe she hooked up with someone later."

"But why would she do that? She wouldn't have gone off with just anyone. Krista wasn't dumb."

"Maybe it was someone she knew, and trusted."

Meg shook her head. "I still can't believe she's dead."

"I know."

They sat quietly for a minute or so.

"Is it always like this, Mom, when someone dies? How long does it take to believe it? That they're dead?"

Claire took care with her answer. "It is a slow process. You never lose the person. They slowly become someone you can no longer have in your life."

"I don't want this to be happening. I would do anything to make it be three days ago when Krista and I were getting ready for the party."

"Yeah, I know." Claire started the car. "I'm going out to tell her parents. Whoever gave her the methamphetamine would be considered responsible for her death."

Meg grabbed her backpack and opened the door. "She should have been with me. Then she'd be alive."

She scrambled out of the car, then turned back and said, "It's still my fault."

CHAPTER 10

3 p.m.

Amy climbed into the big orange safety overalls. They were clumsy to work in, but mandatory in a situation like this. She walked away from her squad car feeling as if she were enveloped in a paper bag. Maybe this was how women felt in those burquas—lost and flopping around.

The overalls made a crinkly noise when she walked. They reminded her of wearing a pumpkin costume for Halloween. The face mask was already fogging up and causing her to sweat. But she knew she needed to wear it to protect herself as she was digging in the remains of the trailer. Even with the mask on, as she walked closer to the site, she could smell the distinctive cat-pee reek of a meth lab.

The proliferation of methamphetamines had changed how the police worked—made everything harder and more dangerous. She shuddered when she thought of herself standing on the edge of the yard two days ago, watching the trailer burn. She didn't want to know what carcinogens she had breathed in just standing there.

Not to mention the firefighters who were on the scene. The county couldn't afford to get them the safety equipment they needed. Plus when you rush to a fire how do you know it's going to turn out to be a meth house. They can look like the cutest little cottage in the country. More often a trashed-out trailer, but you never knew.

Amy stood on the edge of the burn zone and looked down at the scorched outlines of where the trailer had been, only some of the exterior walls still standing. She could make out the rooms as if a pretend house had been drawn on the ground. Her assignment was to pick out any salvageable pieces of cooking equipment and bag it to send to forensics.

As she walked in to the remains of the trailer, she wondered what she was looking for and why. What more would they learn from this conflagration? It was obvious what had been going on in the small trailer.

Amy could easily imagine the scenario—Letty brewing up a batch of meth, probably puts the lid on too tight and the pot of chemicals blows catching the kitchen on fire. The fire gets out of control, happens so fast she can't get out of the trailer. Or worse she stays and tries to save the meth because she needs it so badly, not wanting to call for help because she doesn't want to get arrested.

There had been no call from the scene. The firefighters had been alerted by a neighbor driving by who had seen the fire.

Thank god Letty's little boy had been staying at Arlene's. The only thing that made Letty a good mom was the sense to get that kid out of the trailer when she was making meth so he hadn't died too.

The metal of the stove was scorched black but discernible up against the front wall of the trailer. A large stainless steel pot was turned upside down by the door. That must have been what she had been using to cook the meth.

Amy stepped out of the charred remains of the trailer and walked back toward the woods. If this scene were like other meth houses, she knew what she would find. She didn't have to walk far. Not even into the woods. Right in the middle of the field she found garbage bags full of meth debris: old jugs and bottles, used rubber gloves, gas cans, old boxes of Sudafed, camper fluid. Mixed in were dirty diapers, empty beer cans, and paper plates with crusted moldy food.

After ripping a bag or two open, Amy decided she had seen enough. It was time to call in hazardous-materials specialists from the state. She knew they would dispose of this stuff in special landfills.

As Amy walked back to the car, she thought about Letty, who she had known since they were in their teens, although Letty was older than her. Letty didn't seem strong enough or smart enough to brew up a batch of methamphetamines by herself. Plus, the woman never did anything unless there was a guy involved.

Only one body had been found in the trailer, but Amy didn't believe that Letty had been alone.

***

3:30 p.m.

Jared woke with his body as stiff as a board, all his muscles tight with the need for some crank.

Waking up is hardly what he would call his entrance back into the world—it felt more like he had been dropped full belly flop onto rock-hard ground, his whole body screaming in pain.

Two days without any meth, the longest he had been without in awhile. The only reason he made it that long was that he had slept most of the time. The only thought he had was how to get some meth.

If he could crawl out of bed, he felt like he would do anything to get it.

Where was Hitch? That was the question. Jared knew of a couple other guys that might be able to get him some crank, but they were neither reliable nor easy to get hold of. He needed to find Hitch.

He held up his hands and saw how thin and bruised they were, saw how they shook like aspen leaves in a light breeze. He couldn't deal with that now. He couldn't believe how much he hurt. His head pounded until it felt like his brain would burst out of his skull, all his muscles ached, and his feet throbbed.

Then he got hit with a really horrible thought—Hitch might well have skipped the county, the state for that matter. Lately, he had been complaining about the Mexicans coming in and taking over his territory, selling imported meth for less than he could make it.

This thought poked at Jared until he sat up in bed and then tried to stand, but he couldn't seem to move his feet.

He crashed to the floor.

Seconds later his mother pushed open the door. Davy peeked around her legs. The two of them stared at him from the doorway.

"Was at?" Davy asked, pointing at him.

His mother patted the little boy's head reassuringly. "You know him. That's your cousin, Jared."

"Was matter?"

"He's not feeling so good I'd guess."

His mother came and bent over him, putting an arm under his elbow. She helped him back onto the bed. Thank god he was wearing boxer shorts and a t-shirt. He hated for her to see him like this, but at least he wasn't naked.

"Hungry?" she asked.

Jared shook his head.

"I made your favorite, caramel rolls."

The thought of food still made him queasy. He had to get out of the house. Any excuse. "I need to go to school, Mom."

"No, don't worry. I took care of that. I called in sick for you."

He looked up at her. "You did?"

"You're in no shape to go anyplace. Plus I need you here. I want you to help me with Letty's funeral."

For a flash Jared remembered Letty running back into the trailer. She hadn't made it back out. He wasn't surprised. "She's dead?"

"Yes."

"I'm sorry, Mom."

His mother folded in on herself for a moment, then she straightened. "What happened over there?"

Jared couldn't bring himself to tell her the truth. "Just one of those things. We were in the kitchen and all of a sudden there was a big explosion. I think the stove blew up. Probably a gas leak."

"You were making that stuff." She didn't say it as a question.

He said nothing.

"Well, even though there's not much left of her, we need to bury her. She was my sister. There's no one else left to do it."

"When?"

"In a couple days."

"Maybe I should go over there, check on the trailer," Jared suggested, thinking this might be a way to get out of the house. "Could I take your car?"

"Don't worry about that trailer. Good riddance. I don't think there's anything left of it. What you need to do is eat. You must be starving after all that sleeping. If you don't want rolls what do you want?"

"Nothing, Mom. I need to get out of here." Jared stood up again and tried to walk, but his legs still wouldn't move. This time he looked down at his feet and couldn't believe what he saw.

His old bike chain was wrapped tightly around his ankles and then padlocked to the bed. "What the hell ...?"

***

5 p.m.

Bridget answered the phone, "Wabasha Pharmacy."

"Hey, it's me. I'm sorry to call you at work, but I'm having a hard time here. I need to understand what goes on with meth a little better." Claire often checked in with her sister about drug-related issues. As a pharmacy intern Bridget had worked at a Poison Control center and a drug-rehab treatment program.

"I've got a minute. We're kinda slow today."

"So tell me what you know about methamphetamine."

"Meth is bad."

"I think I know that."

"Extremely addictive. The figure I remembered from school that astounded me was that over a six-month period 94 percent of users that smoked it got addicted."

"Yikes. Why?"

"Well, meth is a stimulant. From what I hear it makes you feel very, very good. Like there's nothing you can't do. It has a similar high to cocaine only longer and stronger. Where a cocaine high might last a half an hour, meth can last for eight to twelve hours. In the process it depletes the epinephrine in the body. And then the user wants more."

"A first-time user, might they want to kill themselves?"

"Highly unlikely. But they might try to do something that they can't do and end up dead."

"Yeah, that's what I was afraid of. Thanks." Claire then told Bridget what she was afraid had happened to Krista.

Bridget said how sorry she was.

When Claire hung up the phone, she felt weary and hid her head in her arms on the desk. Sometimes the job weighed a lot.

After a moment, she felt a tap on her shoulder.

"You okay?" Amy's broad sweet face looked down at her.

"I went out to the Jorgenson's again."

Amy pushed back some papers and perched on the edge of Claire's desk. "They're taking it really hard, huh?"

"Unspeakably hard. When I did this in the cities, told people how their kids had died, I didn't know them. My daugher wasn't best friends with their daughter. It could have been Meg."

"It can't have been suicide. Krista was such a happy-go-lucky kid. It was a probably an accident. Goofing off."

Claire sadly shook her head. "You haven't heard the latest news. I got a call on the autopsy. Evidence of meth in her bloodwork."

Amy stood up so suddenly she sent a rush of paper sliding off the desk. Neither one of them did anything about the papers. "Meth? What the hell is going on here? Looks like this county has caught the meth disease just when I thought we might escape the worst of it. That trailer that burned? Meth lab."

"Didn't you say that a body was found in there?"

"Yes, Letty Crandall. She's been a well-known tweaker for the last few years so it should come as no surprise, but I never thought she was cooking the stuff. Sad story. She used to be a real beauty. I think she was even homecoming queen. Dark hair, great figure. She was a few years older than me which would make her about thirty now. Last time I saw her in Durand, I thought I was looking at a sixty-year-old bag lady. I kid you not. She was so skinny and haggard."

Amy shook her head. "The good news is her three-year-old kid was at her sister's when the fire happened. So at least he's still alive."

"He should probably be checked out for methamphetamine exposure."

"I'll tell Arlene. The thing is I'm sure that Letty was working with someone else, some guy. That's who I want to find."

"Maybe we should go talk to this sister."

"Okay. The funeral's tomorrow—let's wait until after that."

"Krista's funeral is tomorrow too," Claire said.

"How's Meg doing with all this?" Amy asked. Amy and Meg had met when Amy had dropped over some paperwork a few months ago. Claire hadn't been home yet and they started talking about music and the coolest blogs.

When Claire had seen how well the two of them got along it underscored the fact that Amy was much closer in age to Meg than to Claire. Claire was nearly fifty, Amy was twenty-three and Meg was fifteen. Maybe Amy could give her some advice on what to do to help Meg get through this tough time.

"Meg's taking it so hard, it's kinda scaring me. She's totally blaming herself and I don't seem to be able to talk sense into her."

"Well, maybe she's not ready for sense yet. Maybe you should try agreeing with her."

Claire lifted her head. "You think?"

Amy shrugged. "It's worth a try. I remember my mom doing that to me. I'd come home from school and whine and say how fat I was. She'd look me up and down and say, 'You're not exactly fat, but you could stand to lose a couple pounds.' It sure shut me up and made me look at myself. Listen, having Meg upset about her friend's death from meth might not be such a bad thing if it keeps her from ever trying the crap."

CHAPTER 11

November 4, 11 p.m.

When Claire slipped into a pew right by the door of the church, she found herself sitting next to the Bakkes, who owned the gas station in Fort St. Antoine. Grace Bakke, blond hair spun into a cotton-candy-like shape, whispered, "This is such a very sad day for us all."

Grace could go on for a good long while if you gave her a chance so Claire just nodded.

"Krista was a lovely girl," Grace said, then she couldn't help adding, "But a little wild."

"Yes," Claire said with an edge in her voice. To herself she said, Give her nothing. The woman will just repeat it all over town.

"How's Meg taking it?" Grace continued.

"About as expected." Claire turned away to see if she could find her daughter and Rich.

Way up at the front, she made out the backs of Rich's and Meg's heads. She thought of trying to push her way through the crowd and sit with them, but decided it would be too much work and she wasn't sure there was any room in the pew.

The small country church was overflowing, people standing all along the sides of the aisles and out the front steps. She was lucky to have found a seat. More than half the people in the church were kids. She knew the school had closed for the afternoon to let all the students come to the funeral. They would have come anyway.

The Almalund Moravian Church's simple interior gave Claire a sense of peace whenever she was there, which wasn't often. The walls were painted a salmon color, the windows simple stained glass. A plain wooden cross, the size of a man, hung over the altar.

As the pastor entered the sacristy, the organist started playing the hymn, "Abide with Me." Everyone stood and sang. The sound of so many voices raised together in the small church was like a clean wind coming across newly planted fields.

Claire tried to pay attention to the service, but as she so often did, when the sermon started, she slipped away into her own thoughts: this time about her daughter and what might have happened to her best friend. More than ever she wanted to know what had made Krista jump off the cliff. She didn't believe—whatever it was—it had anything to do with Meg. But she knew she wouldn't be able to persuade Meg of that—Meg would have to come to it herself.

After the sermon, the pastor announced that Krista's father, Roger Jorgenson, would like to say a few words.

As Roger stood, Claire noticed how much he had aged in the past few days. She had seen it before when people grieved, but was still shocked by his transformation. He seemed to have collapsed in on himself.

His tall body sagged, grief pulling every muscle and bone toward the ground, slowing his steps, blurring his eyes. Some of his spirit had been stolen when his daughter died.

As he walked up to the lectern to speak, Roger looked so unsteady Claire was afraid that he might fall. Although he tottered, he righted himself and, after setting down a piece of paper, grabbed both edges of the wooden lectern and stood taller.

"Friends and neighbors, thanks for coming today." He cleared his throat and looked down at the piece of paper that he had laid on the lectern. "You all know our eldest daughter died this last week, Krista Ellen Jorgenson. I can't tell you," he bowed his head for a second, then continued, "how much we're going to miss her.

"Krista was a good kid and helped around the farm. She especially liked to gather the eggs in the morning. She kept track of how many eggs she found every day. I don't know why, but she liked to do that." He bent his head and wiped at his face.

Claire heard sobs breaking out in the audience and felt the pressure of tears build in her eyes.

Slowly Roger Jorgenson shook his head. "I do not want to be here today. I would rather be any place else. I'm not one for talking to crowds. I'm a farmer. But I can't stay silent."

He spoke more loudly. "My daughter was murdered."

Claire felt the hair rise on the back of her neck.

"She is not the only one. People are being killed in our county. Not just adults, but teenagers. Our children are being killed by this horrible drug—methamphetamine. We must stop it."

Roger stared out at his audience. "You think you can ignore this problem. You think it has nothing to do with you. I know, that's how I felt. You know something weird's going on at that old trailer down the road. You think someone's been siphoning ammonia hydroxide from your tank, but you don't bother to report it. You know, but you don't say anything. You keep silent.

You don't want to get involved. Well, I'm here to ask you to get involved."

Roger shook his head. "Krista had just turned sixteen. Many of you had known her all your lives. She had just got her license. She had big plans. She had her whole life ahead of her.

"If any of you kids know anything about what happened that night, I want you to tell me or the police. I will not stop until I find out who was responsible for my daughter taking this drug. Whoever gave it to her, killed her. It's as simple as that." He looked out at the crowd. "I'm asking for your help. Thank you."

There was silence, punctuated with the occasional sniffle as Roger slowly made his way down the stairs to his seat, bent over once again.

***

12 p.m.

Rich nodded at neighbors, shook hands with old farmers and friends, but didn't see Claire any place. He and Meg walked out of the church and down the steps. Meg hunched inside her jacket, not meeting anyone's eye.

"Where's Mom? She said she would be here," Meg asked Rich as they stood out on the lawn and watched people come out of the church. Warm for a fall day, the wind smelled of burnt leaves.

"She's probably gone already. She told me this morning that she wasn't positive she could get away for the funeral and if she did, I don't think she was planning on staying afterwards."

Meg snapped, "She can't even take time off to stick around at the funeral. Krista's funeral. I hate it that she's a cop."

Rich didn't answer. No sense in pointing out that Claire was probably working to solve Krista's death. Meg would only get more angry. There were no good responses to Meg's thrashing these days.

"You want to go back in for the luncheon," Rich suggested.

Meg shook her head.

"We need to eat." Rich had been looking forward to the meal the church ladies would have set out: hot dishes of every variety, salads and bars.

"I'm not hungry. I don't want to see anybody. I just want to go home."

"What about me? What if I'm hungry?" Rich asked gently.

Meg snapped out of her funk for a second and a hint of a smile lit on her lips, then she said, "You do go for that tuna casserole in a big way."

"As long as it's noted that I have made a big sacrifice for you, we can go home."

When they reached the car, Rich asked, "You want to drive?"

Meg had her permit and begged to drive everywhere they went. He thought it might take her mind off of the funeral for a moment. He hated how hard she was being on herself for Krista's death. Sadness was one thing, but blaming herself the way she was could be damaging.

To his surprise Meg nodded. He tossed the keys over to her and they got into the car. She backed the car up very carefully, checking both sides.

She drove through the farmland and Rich relaxed in his seat. Meg was getting to be a pretty good driver. He just hoped she wouldn't pick up any of the bad habits people learned driving these empty country lanes, like driving in the middle of the road unless someone was coming from the other direction.

As they started down the hill toward Fort St. Antoine, Rich thought Meg's foot was a little heavy on the pedal, but he didn't say anything. It was good for her to learn these things on her own. He found his foot pumping the floor on the passenger side. A lot of good that would do. But Meg was making the curves without too much trouble so he kept quiet.

As she came down to Highway 35 she didn't slow up enough to make the last turn and a whoop came out of his mouth as she headed across the steep road and managed to aim the car onto a deeply rutted field road.

Grass ticked at the underside of the car carriage and she stopped the vehicle before it went into the field.

"I think I was going a little too fast," Meg said without looking over at him.

"I think so."

Meg didn't say anything for a second. She turned off the car and they sat in silence. "Maybe I shouldn't be driving."

"No, this is how you learn. You'll be fine if you slow down a bit. The car's okay. We're fine. Could have done a lot worse."

"I don't do anything right anymore." Meg blubbered. Tears poured down her face as she sank back into the seat. The crying turned into wailing, then long sobs tore out of her throat.

Rich let her cry. She needed to get it out of her. She had kept all this sadness bottled up inside of her and it wouldn't let her alone. When she started to throttle down, he patted her shoulder. She turned toward him and he hugged her.

"Rich, what am I going to do?"

"About what?"

She pulled away and looked at him, her eyes red and swollen from crying, her face splotched. "About my life. It's all ruined. I don't know what to do."

He knew it would do no good to tell her that she would get through this horrible time. No teenager should have to feel responsible for the death of their best friend.

"Do you really want my advice?" Rich asked.

She sniffled and nodded.

"You need to focus on one thing at a time. And right now I think you need to back up slowly and get us home. That's enough for you to do right now."

"But," Meg wiped her face. "I think I should try to find out who gave Krista the meth."

"That's not your job." Rich decided not to mention that it was her mother's job. Meg seemed to be down on Claire these days.

"But I could ask around. Like Mr. Jorgenson said. Someone's gotta know who she was with."

"Is there anyone in your school who you think is doing meth?"

"I don't know," she said. "There might be someone I could talk to …" She cut herself off and started the car.

Rich hung onto the seatbelt as Meg hit reverse hard and the car bumped out onto the road, then headed toward home.

***

1 p.m.

Amy hadn't known what to wear to Letty's funeral.

She decided she wasn't going to go in her uniform even if it meant she'd have to change out of it and back into it at work. She was going to this funeral as a civilian and felt it was improper to wear her deputy sheriff uniform. Plus she knew it would make people ill at ease and have them assume she was there on official business.

So she chose a pair of black slacks, using a roll of duct tape to get the cat hairs off of them, and a dark jacket over a black turtleneck. Sitting in the squad car outside the brick church in Durand, she craned her neck to look into her rearview mirror. Lipstick would help. Digging through the bottom of her purse, she found a tube of "Ripe Plum." Sounded good. She applied it, careful to get none on her teeth as she smiled at herself in the mirror.

When she walked into the church, she remembered how ugly this old building was. Dark paneling made it seem smaller than it was and cheap light fixtures threw a dim light. The one stained glass window over the altar was framed into a box with artificial light shining behind it. Amy thought the whole point of stained glass was to have the sun shine through the colored glass to remind people of the light of God.

The church was crowded; she recognized many people from high school. She slid into the only pew left, which was close to the front.

Amy didn't recognize the family sitting next to her in the pew. As she glanced over at them, she wondered why she had worried about what she was wearing. The father was dressed in full camouflage gear. The really sad thing was it was probably his best outfit. His wife wore jeans and a sweatshirt that said Green Bay Packers. The two boys at least had their hair slicked back in an attempt at civility. Amy wondered if they were some of Letty's new friends since she had dropped out of the regular world.

The organist was fumbling her way through some old hymn but no one paid her much attention as they talked amongst themselves. Amy checked the time and saw that there was still a few minutes before the service would start.

The front-row pew reserved for the family was still empty. She felt so sorry for Arlene. She was such a good woman and had lost her husband only a few years ago. Now she had lost her only sister and in such a dreadful way.

Amy knew there would be no coffin. There had been little left of Letty's body and the family had decided to cremate. A silver urn stood on a small table at the bottom of the stairs going up to the altar.

Letty's high school picture in a dark frame stared out at the crowd. With her large eyes and dark hair, she had been a pretty woman and full of life until she started to do drugs.

A bouquet of dyed blue carnations was next to the urn with what looked like a blue velvet hat tucked into the bouquet.

Amy swallowed a laugh. Why had they stuck an old hat in the bouquet? Whose idea was that? The style of the hat showed that it was probably from Letty's teens, maybe something she had worn for Easter. Some small personal memento of a life gone terribly wrong. How do you make sense of what had happened to Letty?

As the organist turned up the volume and pumped hard into "Onward Christian Soldiers," three people came walking up the aisle: Arlene, Letty's son Davy, and Jared.

Arlene led the way in a dark navy suit and looked fairly composed. Davy was dancing at her side, too young to understand what was going on. He had on a dark suit coat that looked too big for him. Probably a hand-me-down of Jared's. He was carrying a book with him. Amy guessed it was to keep him quiet during the service.

On the other side of the small boy, also holding his hand, was Jared. He walked very unsteadily.

Amy remembered Jared when he had been a little older than Davy.

She had babysat him when she was in high school, and he was about six or seven. He had been such a sweet kid, so interested in everything. She would often practice her Spanish when she was babysitting and he loved to sit and listen to her talk Spanish. He thought it was magic that she could speak another language. He would ask her word after word, "how do you say horse? how do you say potato?"

But now Amy just stared at Jared. He must be about the age she had been when she babysat him, in his late teens. She hadn't seen him in years. But she recognized the look he had.

Since she had taken the meth workshop at the end of her law enforcement program, Amy saw this look everywhere she went: on people putting in two dollars worth of gas in their junkie cars, getting prescriptions at pharmacies, trying to take the edge off by drinking beer late at night in the bars.

She called them zombies, the walking dead. Emaciated, way past skinny. Sunken faces the result of teeth rotting away. No flicker in their eyes.

To her they looked like what she imagined zombies would be—fueled solely by a burning desire to feed the small fire that burned at the core of them—the need to have more meth. They wanted nothing else out of life. They cared for no one, not even themselves.

So when Jared came walking down the aisle of the church at his aunt's funeral, Amy knew what he was—a meth freak.

CHAPTER 12

3 p.m.

"How was your funeral?" Amy asked as she sat down at her desk kitty-corner from Claire's.

Claire shook her head, remembering the sadness wafting through the church like incense gone bad. A young person's funeral was always depressing. In this small county, where everyone knew everyone, knew them since they were born, such a death punched a real hole in the community.

"Bleak. I left right after. I couldn't take anymore. I felt guilty that I wasn't at work doing something about Krista's death. Mr. Jorgenson got up and told everyone that his daughter had been murdered. He said that whoever gave her the meth had killed her. I have to agree with him." She twisted her legs around each other and looked at Amy. "How was yours?"

"One of the stranger ones I've been too." Amy paused, then emphasized, "I mean, I grew up here. I know these folks. Do people no longer know what's good manners? This guy was there wearing camouflage. I don't think people have to wear only black to a funeral, but at least to dress up a little in darker clothes. No jeans either. Is that asking too much?"

"I hear ya."

Amy sat down in a rolling chair across the desk from Claire. "But the other thing I figured out at the funeral is, after seeing young Jared, I just got this very strong hint that he's doing meth."

"Really? Jared? He goes to school with Meg. I think he's a grade or two ahead of her. What makes you think that?"

"You know, you just can tell. Skinny, bad complexion. He hasn't been on it long enough to lose his teeth, but that will happen if he continues."

"Did you talk to him? About Krista?"

"I decided to wait. A funeral just didn't seem like the place. I can do that today. After the meeting with the sheriff. He said ten after," Amy tilted her head toward the clock.

They both stood up and walked into Sheriff Talbert's office. He had a pair of reading glasses on that made him look older than Claire usually thought of him. He kept reading but when Bill Trudeau came in he took the glasses off and motioned them all to sit. Claire and Amy took the chairs and Bill leaned against the wall.

The sheriff said, "Krista Jorgenson's once-thought-to-be-accidental death might well turn into a murder investigation. I want to be ready if that happens. Claire will be looking into it. I want the two of you, Amy and Bill, to help her out however you can. At the moment, we're going to keep it in-house, but if we need more help, I'll call in the crime bureau."

The three deputy sheriffs nodded.

"What've you got, Claire?"

"The meth angle is what we need to figure out. There's a good chance that Krista died because someone gave her some meth." Claire cleared her throat. She tried not to think of the bright Krista she had known. "But we still don't know what happened—if she fell, if she jumped or even if she was pushed. We might never know."

"Was she a known user?"

"Quite the contrary. Her parents swore up and down, when I told them there had been meth in her blood, that she had never done it before. Most parents don't know what's going on with their kids. But, as you know, my daughter Meg was her best friend. And she claims that Krista had never done any drugs. Not coke, not grass, nothing. She says Krista would have a beer or two, but didn't even like wine or hard liquor. They talked about drugs—but Krista said she had never touched anything. No reason for her to lie to Meg." Claire pulled her hair back.

"I assume Meg's reliable. She wouldn't be trying to protect her dead friend, would she?"

"My daugher's not perfect, but she doesn't lie."

Amy piped in. "She's a good kid. I'd trust her with my cat."

The sheriff pushed himself back from his desk and blew out air. "Well, I heard about what Roger Jorgenson said at his daughter's funeral. A number of people have called me about it, telling me they've been missing anhydrous ammonia, asking me to find the meth pushers around here and stop them. Wish it were that easy. In a way it doesn't matter how she fell to her death: if it was an accident or if she jumped on purpose, because whoever gave her the meth basically killed her just as sure as if he had pushed her off that cliff, which he might have done."

"Statute 609.195 states you give someone a controlled substance and they die, you're guilty of murder in the third degree," Amy reeled off.

Bill looked over at her and smirked. "Can always tell the rookies cause they still know the numbers to all the laws."

"So let's start looking harder at the meth dealers in this county, the ones we know about, find out what other ones are out there. Hopefully the phone calls will keep coming in with more info. Give us some good leads," the sheriff said and then dismissed them.

The three of them left the office and stood in the hallway talking. "We just sent two guys up from Monona. I'll ask around," Bill said.

"I was thinking maybe we should talk to Margie." Amy suggested to Claire, ignoring Bill. "She's in the jail. Do you know who she is?"

"I don't think so."

"She's a skinny blond. Looks like she's about ten, but I think she's over twenty. Maybe old enough to drink. Not a juvie, that's for sure. She knows more about the world than you and I put together."

"I know who you mean," Bill said. "Kinda cute if you like the beat-up look."

Once again Amy ignored Bill, which made Claire wonder if there was something going on between those two.

"When they brought her in here she slept for five days straight. I helped turn her from side to side so she wouldn't get bed sores."

"How long has she been here?" Claire asked.

"Two weeks. She's still buggy and shaking. Picks at her scalp. Can't seem to stop. But she's finally on the docket."

"What's she in for—possession?" Claire asked.

"No, she broke into a one of those big houses on the top of the bluff. Unlucky for her the owners had an alarm."

Bill started laughing. "I took that call. When Jed and I got there we found her in the closet off the master bedroom, trying on clothes. Not too smart."

"Well, you guys weren't too smart to strip search her. You know a woman is supposed to be present."

"No way we strip searched her. We just told her to take off the woman's clothes. We had to stay and watch her so she didn't try anything."

Claire said, "I don't want to hear about this. Let's get to work. Bill, you track down those guys and find out anything you can on the dealers in the area. Amy and I will go talk to Margie and let's meet later to compare notes."

After Bill walked away, Claire turned and asked Amy, "What's up with you and Bill?"

"I don't like how he's always throwing in my face how new I am to all this. Plus, I don't think he always plays by the rules."

"He's a good deputy."

"Maybe it's just that I was taught how to do everything by the book. Out in the field I suppose you have to be more relaxed."

When they opened the thick door to her cell, Margie was sitting on the edge of her bed, rocking and humming. Her long dark blond hair hung over her face, but patches of her scalp showed, scabbed over. On her hands were a pair of mittens. She didn't look up when the two women entered her cell.

Amy wondered if the girl needed some psychiatric help. She looked so withdrawn. "Margie, can we ask you a few questions?"

The thin girl shrugged, her shoulders lifting the orange prison outfit, but she still didn't look at them.

"This is Claire. She's another deputy sheriff. We had a girl jump off a cliff under the influence of meth, her first time taking it, and we want to ask you some questions about where she might have gotten the stuff."

"She die?" Margie asked, little inflection in her voice.

"She did."

"Lucky her."

"Why do you say that?" Claire asked.

"Then she'll never end up here." Margie added with more enthusiasm, "Plus the first time is the best. Imagine going out on that."

"When was your first time?" Amy asked, wanting to keep her talking.

"I was seventeen. Seems like a million years ago. I was in love with this guy and he had some glass. He said it was primo. I tried it. The guy and I broke up a few months later, but I kept doing the meth."

"How often?"

"Started out about twice a week. Then more. Then all the time."

"Where'd you get it?"

"Around. Wherever I could."

"You didn't have one dealer."

"Not exactly. I could get it from guys pretty easy. You know, trade 'em for it. A little sex for a little crank."

"Can you give us any names of any guys who are dealing?"

"A guy named Hitch is selling around here. Although a lot of crap is coming in from Mexico."

"Is that his first name or his last?"

Margie gave a hoarse laugh. "You've gotta be kidding. This isn't like a social event when you're buying crank. All I know is that's what everyone calls him. Hitch."

"Do you know where he is—this Hitch guy?"

"Last I heard he was shacked up with Letty in her trailer out on double D."

Amy and Claire looked at each other. Funny how it was all circling around that trailer fire.

"That trailer burned down. Can you think of any other place he might be?"

Margie didn't even pause long enough to think. She started shaking her head and her hair covered her face. "Don't know."

"Thanks, Margie. If you think of anything else, please let us know."

As they were turning to leave, Margie finally lifted up her head. Claire stared at her. She had the face of an angel. Soft blue eyes, full pink lips, a kind of innocence not often seen in a teenager.

"Hey," Margie said. "I think I should see a doctor."

"What's going on?" Amy asked. "You still having a hard time coming off the meth?"

"Yes, but that's not it." She paused, wet her lips with her tongue, then said, "My period's late."

***

4 p.m.

Meg stared down at her cousin Rachel, sleeping in her lap. The little girl had fallen asleep while Meg was reading to her from a favorite book. Rachel had only just turned three but, because she was small for her age, she still fit in Meg's lap. That wouldn't be the case for much longer.

Earlier that day, Bridget had called to see if Meg could babysit for an hour or two. Rich, acting "en loco parentis," said she could.

Meg knew that she could have gently moved Rachel to the couch and watched TV or something, but she just sat there with the child sprawled across her lap. Penance. Everything seemed like penance.

If I'm just good enough for the rest of my life, maybe I'll make up for what I did to Krista, was the way she thought about it.

Just when she didn't think she could sit still anymore, Bridget's car pulled into the driveway. Meg stood up carefully and tried to settle Rachel into the couch, but the little girl stirred and woke.

"Is at my mommy?"

"Yes, indeed, it is."

"You going home?"

"Pretty soon."

Bridget came in hauling two bags of groceries. After depositing the bags on the coffee table, she hugged both of them at the same time. "My two favorite girls," she said.

Rachel snuggled back into the couch, popped her thumb in her mouth and closed her eyes again.

"How'd it go?" Bridget asked.

"She's an angel."

"Hardly."

"She was today."

"I told her to be good, that cousin Meg was having a hard time."

Bridget carted her bag of groceries into the kitchen and Meg followed. "You have time for a drink?"

"Sure. Nothing too exciting waiting for me back home."

Bridget grabbed two ginger ales out of the refrigerator and they both sat up on stools at the counter. "I haven't talked to you since the funeral. How're you doing?"

"I can see why people do drugs," Meg said, partly to shock her aunt and partly because it was true. "I don't want to be here and I don't want to feel this way. I'd take almost anything to stop feeling so bad."

"Yup, there are times when drugs do help. I wouldn't have a job otherwise."

"Have you ever done drugs, Aunt Bridget?"

"What do you mean by that? Have I ever taken an illegal substance?"

"Yes." Meg realized she wasn't sure how her aunt would answer.

Bridget took a long swallow of ginger ale, then tapped the top of the can with her fingernail. "I guess you're old enough to know this. I did some speed many long years ago to help me study when I was in college. Wouldn't recommend it. But that was a long time ago and I haven't done anything since I got my Pharm Degree."

"You did speed? But you're nearly a doctor."

"I am a doctor. But doctors can be bad substance abusers. Don't tell your mom about this conversation. In fact, forget I even told you."

"Did you like it?"

"Yes and no. It made me anxious and jittery, but I did get my work done."

"What was it like?"

"Like chugging a huge pot of coffee. Made me feel like my skin was stretched too tight over my body."

"Thanks for telling me."

"Why do you ask?"

"You heard about Krista, that she did meth before she died?"

"Yes, your mom told me. I'm really sorry."

"I've just been wondering about it. What she felt and all."

"Well, meth is a whole nother story. Baddest stuff out there. Worse than heroin in many ways. More addictive. Don't even think about it."

"I wasn't," Meg lied.

***

10 p.m.

Stretched out on the bed, Rich watched Claire folding her laundry. She folded clothes the way she did most everything—slow and steady. After he had dyed some of her underwear blue by putting it in with his jeans, they had decided that each of them should do their own laundry. Now that Meg was old enough, she did her own too.

Claire continued to talk about her day, how Margie had asked to see a doctor. "I pray she's not pregnant. She's not old enough to take care of herself. She's totally fucked up from the meth. She doesn't need a kid now."

"Who knows. Might pull her together."

Claire stopped and looked over at him. Rich wouldn't call the glare on her face one of complete disgust, but it was full of disdain. "That kind of risk is not worth a child's life."

Rich shrugged.

Claire continued, snapping t-shirts as she talked. "This kid has picked half her head raw. She weighs about twenty pounds. She has no home, didn't finish school, no job, no support, probably facing a jail sentence. I wouldn't doubt she has brain damage from her drug use. One of the many times I think an abortion is in order. This is not the time to have a baby."

"I agree." Rich knew not to argue with her when she was in this mood.

Claire finished folding the last shirt and took a deep breath. "So how was Meg today?"

Rich had already decided he wasn't going to tell her about Meg driving off the road and into a field. "I think she did okay. She didn't want to stay at the funeral, but I wasn't surprised. When she got home, she asked if she could go for a walk in the woods. I let her. Bridget called later and wanted her to watch Rachel. That okay?"

"Of course. Might be good for her to be around Bridget. She might open up more with her than me."

Claire put the last of her clothes away in the drawer, then slid in bed next to him. "How is she ever going to get over this?"

"Slowly." Rich put an arm around her. His book was resting on his chest. "I think it has helped her to learn about the meth. Given her something else to focus on. She said she's going to ask around school."

"Good."

Claire leaned in to kiss him goodnight. She smelled like lemons. Must be her shampoo. He sniffed her neck. "You're my drink of lemonade. Sweet and sour at the same time."

She kissed him hard, then pulled back, "Hey, do you know anybody named Hitch?"

Rich thought for a moment. That name did sound familiar. "There was a guy that played football over in Monona. He was a lot younger than me. Think his name was Ben Hitchcock. He came from a big family other side of Durand. Could be one of his siblings. Or him."

CHAPTER 13

November 5, 7:30 a.m.

Amy shivered in the early morning cool as she slipped into the squad car parked in her driveway. The car thermometer said the outside temperature was only 35 degrees. She snuggled further into her jacket. Another hard frost last night. About right for early November. As she drove to town, she noticed most of the leaves were down, except for the oaks.

She decided to stop off at Arlene's before she went to the sheriff's department. Might be a good idea to catch her in the morning before she'd had too much coffee. Maybe Jared wouldn't have left for school yet and she could talk to him too.

As she pulled up in front of the bungalow on the outskirts of Durand, Amy could tell that Arlene was having a hard time keeping up her home since her husband died. It showed in the little things: a window screen hanging loose, tiny trees growing out of the gutter, paint peeling under the windows.

The door swung open before Amy had a chance to knock. Arlene backed out of the house wearing a pink chenille bathrobe and carrying a recycling container full of cans and bottles. When she saw Amy she jumped.

"Sorry. Didn't mean to scare you," Amy said, stepping forward and taking the container out of Arlene's arms. "How'd the funeral go? I had to leave early and couldn't stay for the luncheon."

"Amy, thanks. I hardly remember what happened yesterday. It's all been such a blur."

They walked to the curb and Amy put the container down where Arlene pointed.

"I'm so sorry about Letty. It's just a shame. She wasn't that old, was she?"

Arlene pulled her bathrobe tight around herself. "She was in her thirties. Twelve years younger than me. My mom's menopausal surprise."

They walked back to the door and stood there, talking about the funeral: who had been there, who hadn't shown up. Amy could tell that Arlene was getting cold, standing outside in her bathrobe, but she didn't seem to want to invite Amy in.

She'd have to do it herself. "Listen, Arlene, I need to talk to you about what happened to Letty. Can I come in and sit down?"

"Where are my manners? Of course, come on in." Arlene led the way as they entered the house through the kitchen. She walked right to the coffeepot and poured them both a cup of coffee, didn't even bother to ask Amy if she wanted one, just handed it to her black.

"Just what I needed." After taking a sip, Amy said, "Good coffee."

"I figure if you're going to make it every day, it might as well be good. I put an egg in it like my mom did."

Amy sniffed. "An egg?"

"That's the Swedish way. Mellows it out, I guess."

"Where are the boys?" Amy asked.

"Both sleeping."

"Isn't Jared going to school today?"

Arlene looked down at her coffee. "He just hasn't been up to it. He was real close to his aunt. And then that friend of his from school died, Krista. He seemed to take that real hard."

Amy knew that was true. But wondered if that was the real reason he wasn't going to school. "How's he doing?"

"Not great."

Amy wondered what they were talking about. She decided to push Arlene a little, see what she would reveal. "He looked a little rough yesterday."

"He's a good kid. He'll come through it."

Amy wondered if Arlene had guessed at Jared's meth use. She must have. She was no dummy. She knew what her sister had been doing.

Amy pulled out her notebook. "I need to ask you some questions."

"You're going to write them down?"

"Yes, that way I have a record."

"What about?"

Amy figured she'd start with Letty. "I need to know what your sister was up to, who her friends were."

"Why?"

"Arlene, you know what she was doing. We're pretty sure the trailer caught on fire when she was making methamphetamine."

Horror flashed across Arlene's face, and hatred. "I knew that stuff would kill her. It is the devil's work that drug."

"Yes, I think you're right about that. Who did she hang out with?"

Arlene shook her head. "I wish I could tell you, but I don't know. There was one guy I saw a few times. Some creepy biker guy."

"You don't know his name."

"I know it sounds strange, but I don't. I never was introduced to him, just saw him once or twice when I'd stop by."

"Letty never mentioned him?"

"Other than taking Davy whenever she wanted me to, I haven't had much contact with her the last three-four years. She wouldn't quit using that crap and I didn't want to watch her die."

Arlene stroked her hands as if she was pulling on gloves. "I tried to help her. I did everything to get her to treatment, but she wouldn't go." Arlene sobbed as if something was caught in her throat. "She was my sister. I really tried to help her."

"I know you did. Everyone knows you did. There was nothing more you could do. Thank god you had Davy with you."

"Yes, poor little tyke. What am I going to tell him about his mom?"

Amy didn't know the answer. She hated to give Arlene more bad news, but she needed to make sure Arlene understood the danger Davy had been in. "You better have Davy checked out, Arlene. Bring him to the doctor and explain to the doctor what his mom was doing. He could have been exposed to some bad things."

Arlene shook her head. "God. It never ends, does it?"

Jared came walking down the hall. He was wearing a white T-shirt that hung off his thin shoulders and a pair of longjohns. A thick pair of wool socks were on his feet. "What's the matter, Mom?"

He stopped when he saw Amy.

"You probably don't remember me," she said.

He shrugged his shoulders.

"I babysat you when you were about seven."

He looked at her again, then gave a quick smile. "Oh, yeah. You spoke Spanish. I remember."

Arlene stood up and poured Jared a cup of coffee. He sat down at the table and she set it in front of him. He nearly started to nod off. Arlene nudged him.

"Davy still sleeping?" she asked.

"I guess."

His fingernails were bitten past the quick and looked red and sore. His nose was running and Amy could see a slight tremor in his hand when he reached out for his coffee cup. How was he managing to come off meth on his own? She had watched too many prisoners going through withdrawal, and that was with the help of medication, so she knew how hard it could be. Maybe he hadn't been using too much. That would make it much easier.

Amy decided to jump right in. "What do you know of the fire at Letty's trailer?"

Jared knocked the coffee cup over, the dark brew soaking into the white tablecloth. "Sorry, Mom."

Arlene jumped up to get a sponge and Jared lifted up the cup. When they had settled again, Amy asked, "What do you know, Jared?"

"Nothing. I was here with Mom."

Amy looked at Arlene. The older woman sat with her head down, stirring her coffee. She didn't say anything, but if pushed Amy knew she would say that Jared had been with her. They had closed ranks.

"If I made you give us a blood sample right now, would I find meth in your system?" She decided to scare him.

Jared looked scared. He looked like he was about to bolt. "You can't do that, can you?"

"If we found something of yours at the trailer. If we connect you with what happened at the fire."

"That don't mean nothing. I was over there sometimes."

"You didn't answer the question about the blood sample. You don't look so good, Jared. Have you been taking methamphetamines?"

Jared looked at his mother. She looked away.

"Yeah," Jared whispered. "But I quit. I'm never going to take that shit again. I promised my mom."

"Good for you." Amy continued. Keep asking him questions while he was telling the truth. "Who'd you get the drugs from?"

"A friend of Letty's."

This is what she wanted to hear. "Who?"

"I don't know his real name," Jared mumbled.

"I'm not fooling around here, Jared. I need to know who this guy is."

Jared started, "We always just called him Hitch."

***

11 a.m.

Bill drove back from Monona and watched the fields fly by, golden in their autumn color. His contact hadn't known much more than Margie did. A guy named Hitch was a low-level dealer, mainly cooking for himself, staying under the radar until now. Nothing new.

Bill had wanted to drive back to the sheriff's department, waving this guy Hitch by the neck—impress everyone, especially Amy.

Amy coming to work at the department had changed everything for Bill and he wasn't sure it was for the better. He now understood why many men resisted having women work with them. They just confused things. Sometimes he felt as if he was back in high school. The other problem, he wasn't the only guy in the department who was trying to impress Amy.

The situation had been different when Claire joined the department. She was older and higher up, being appointed chief investigator soon after she had arrived years ago. She had good boundaries, as they said, and kept her distance from them, going home to take care of her daughter. Bill had a lot of respect for Claire.

There was no rule about fraternizing with fellow deputies, hadn't needed one since they were all men up until recently. But Bill just didn't think it was a good idea. He needed to have a clear head and focus on what was going on around him when he was at work, not wondering what this cute woman thought about him.

It didn't help that his former girlfriend had just told him she was getting married to a doctor. She had always wanted money and she had been clear about not wanting to marry a cop. She broke up with him only about six months ago. He still missed her.

And now the sheriff had put Amy and him together with Claire on this case.

Bill drove into the lot and noticed Claire wasn't back yet, but Amy was. He just had to stay professional.

***

11:30 a.m.

"Anybody here by the name of Hitch?"

A whiskered old man with "Herb" sewed onto his shirt sat at the till reading the paper. He looked up at Claire's question and said, "No Hitch, but we've got a Ben Hitchcock. Will that work for you?"

"Sure."

Herb flopped his paper down and pointed to a tall blond man bent over a car. The shoulders gave him away for a former football player. He was leaning over the open engine of a car, crooning to it. "That's it. That's it. Come on, baby. Just turn over once."

Claire stood behind him and waited until he had made the adjustment. Following the lead that Rich had given her, she tracked this Hitchcock down. While she was no expert on methamphetamines, this healthy guy didn't look like he was hooked on them. But he might know something. Or he might be a dead end.

When he turned around, she introduced herself, looking him up and down

"You know anyone that goes by the name of Hitch?" she asked.

He looked her up and down. "You're a cop?"

"That's why I'm wearing the uniform."

He scowled. "Hell, what's he done now?"

"He related to you?"

"Not anymore."

"This Hitch who's no longer related to you, do you know where I might find him?"

"You don't want to find him."

"Why not?"

"He's a sorry excuse for a man. I'm always surprised to hear that he's still alive. Why are you looking for him?"

"A young girl died this last weekend," Claire started.

"Don't tell me," he said.

"I'd like to find Hitch and ask him a few questions about it."

"My dad might know something."

"Where's he?"

"The senior apartments on Main Street."

"Hitch is your brother, right?"

"Was. He's about four years older than me. He was a great older brother. Always watching out for me. Taught me to play pool. Taught me most everything I know about cars. We had big plans. We were going to have our own garage. But that was all before he started doing meth."

"You disown him because of the drugs?"

"No, I hated to see him destroy himself, but he was still my brother. I didn't care if he wanted to take drugs and lose his mind. That's his own business, but he had to tell my mom she could lose some weight on this great stuff. She wasn't even that fat. But she had always been trying to lose weight. I don't think he meant to hurt her. I don't know what he thought he was doing. Hard to tell." Ben shook his head, remembering.

Claire didn't know where he was going with this, but she nodded her head in sympathy.

Ben continued, "So she did a little meth with him. It sure did the trick. She slimmed right down. She never slept. She rarely ate. She thought she looked great. He got our mother hooked on that crap."

"He got her doing meth?"

Ben nodded. "She lost the weight—over a hundred pounds—but that's not all she lost. Two years later she had a heart attack. She died weighing a little over a hundred pounds."

Ben picked up a wrench. "I blame him. As far as I'm concerned, he killed our mother."

"I'm so sorry."

"He's dead to me too," Ben said before he leaned back over the car engine. "That man that's walking around inside his body, I don't know him."

***

3 p.m.

Meg got on the school bus just like she always did after school. She sat next to the window and watched the trees sail by. She missed Krista. It seemed like she missed her friend nearly every moment that she was awake. Once in a while she would forget and think about something else, then this heaviness would drop onto her shoulders and she would wonder why she felt so bad and she would remember. The remembering was awful. Like someone reached inside her mouth, then down her throat and grabbed her heart and pulled on it. That hurtful tug was constantly there, aching and aching.

Meg waved at her house as they passed it. She could see Rich's car in the driveway. She hoped he didn't notice the bus. She had told the bus driver she wanted to get off at a different stop today. She stayed on the bus until Jared's stop.

She had always like Jared. He was two years older than her and she thought he was kinda cool in a long and lanky sort of way. A little like a teenaged Neil Young.

But this year Jared had grown kind of scary, erratic, and out of it. Then he started missing a lot of school. She had heard he might not even be able to graduate. Kids said he was on drugs. They said he was on meth.

A few other kids in school had tried it, but no one else did it steady like Jared. He was supplied by his aunt is what she had heard. Now his aunt was dead. And Krista was dead.

Meg just wanted to find out if Jared knew anything at all about the night that Krista died. One of the kids at the party had said that Jared had showed up for a few minutes toward the end. She figured it was worth a try.

Meg knew where Jared's house was, but had never been inside of it before. She walked up the sidewalk to the bungalow and knocked on the front door. Nothing happened, but she could hear the TV going inside. She knocked louder, trying to be heard over the sound.

The door popped open, but no one was there. Then a small boy poked his head around the edge of the door.

"Hi," Meg said.

"Who are you?" asked the little boy as he held onto the door knob and swung on the door.

"I'm Meg. Who are you?"

"Davy. Davy Gunterson. My mom went far away."

Meg realized this small boy was Jared's Aunt Letty's son. He looked about three years old. "I'm sorry about your mom."

"There's a fire, but I crawled out the window."

"You did?"

"Yeah, and Jared catched me."

Meg hadn't heard that Davy had been at the fire, or Jared. Maybe the small boy was making it up. Maybe he wanted to believe he had been there when his mother died. She understood this feeling. She had imagined Krista's death so many times that she felt like she had been there.

Meg squatted down so her face was at the same height as his face. "You're very lucky."

"I know."

"Can I come in?"

"I'm not supposed to let nobody in."

"Oh, is anyone else here?"

"Yeah, Aunt Arlene and Jared."

"Can you go and get Jared?"

"I'm watching TV."

"If you run it won't take you but a minute."

"Okay, I can run fast." He closed the door in her face.

Meg sat down on the steps.

The door opened again a minute later. Jared's mother was standing behind the screen door, looking down at her. Meg scrambled to her feet.

"I'm a classmate of Jared's. I brought him some homework."

"Oh, that was thoughtful of you. Come on in."

Meg walked in the house and felt rather awkward standing there. Jared's mom invited her into the kitchen and offered her a chair at the table. "Jared should be right down."

When Jared came into the room, he looked like he had just woken up. He was wearing a sweatshirt inside out. Meg guessed he had just pulled it over his head from the way his long brown hair was styled. A pair of jeans completed the outfit. He had on socks, but no shoes.

"Hey," he said.

She wondered if he even knew who she was. Even though their school was small, twenty-five kids in her sophomore class, there wasn't a lot of mixing between the grades. And he was two grades ahead of her. Jared had been one of the cool kids, according to Krista, until this year. Then he had turned into a burn-out.

In school there was a small group of kids that wore black, got tattoos, and pierced their body in odd and inconvenient places. Meg didn't think they all did drugs. In fact, she didn't think most of them did, but the druggies hung out in that group. Jared, if he could be said to hang out with anyone anymore, ganged around with them.

Jared had never paid much attention to her, but they were taking a class together this year. "I brought you some homework from Drama class."

"Thanks." He sat down at the table with her and rubbed his eyes.

"You kids want some pop?" his mom asked.

"I'll take a Coke," Jared said.

"Sure," Meg went along with that. She hardly ever drank soda pop, but she didn't want to be a nuisance.

Jared's mom put two cans of Coke on the table, then said, "I'll be downstairs. I'm just doing the wash."

Meg pulled the homework sheet out of her backpack and handed it to him.

Jared didn't even bother to look at it, saying, "I'm so far behind, I'll never catch up."

"What's going on with you?" Meg took a sip of her Coke just to be polite. She had always found the drink too sweet.

Jared gave her a stare. "What's it to you? What're you doing here anyways? I didn't ask for my homework."

"I know. To tell you the truth I'm trying to find out what happened to Krista. How she died."

At the mention of Krista's name, Jared's head dropped. "Why d'you think I know anything about that?"

"I heard you showed up at the Halloween party after I left. You and some older guy."

"Maybe." Jared lifted the can of Coke and poured the whole thing down his throat as if he were chugging it.

"I don't know if you heard this but Krista had meth in her system when she died. You know anything about that?"

"Shit."

"What?" Meg leaned forward, hoping he would tell her who had given the meth to Krista.

"Nothing."

"Listen. I just want to know for myself. Who gave her the meth? Why did she take it?"

Jared looked her up and down, then looked out at the street. "Did you drive a car here?"

"I can get one." Meg thought about the old pick-up truck sitting alongside the barn at home.

"That'd be great," he said. "I gotta get out of here."

She waited for him to say more. Then she asked the question that no stupid drug workshop had ever really answered for her. "What's it like? Meth?"

He lifted his head, but his eyes were dark and unseeing. "It's like one long roller coaster ride that you never want to end, feeling like you're on top of the world and for the first time can see clearly."

Meg wasn't crazy about roller coasters, but the seeing clearly part, that sounded good. She knew she would like that.

"My mom won't let me go anyplace. She won't let me use her car. I'm like a prisoner. Get me out of here and I'll tell you what I know."

"How can your mom keep you a prisoner?"

Jared looked down at his feet. Meg thought maybe he was embarrassed, then he said, "She's hidden all my shoes."

CHAPTER 14

3 p.m.

Claire walked into Arnold Hitchcock's room in the Bluffland Assisted Living Apartments and found him, wearing a pair of overalls, sitting in the sun and reading the paper with a huge magnifying glass. He was a very large man, solid, not fat, with a large shock of white hair that looked like the mane on a horse.

"Mr. Hitchcock?" she asked.

"That's me, all right." He looked up and squinted. "Can't see so good. They need to fix my cataracts but they're not quite bad enough the doctor says."

She stepped forward and put out her hand. "I'm Claire Watkins, a deputy sheriff here in Pepin County."

When they shook hands, she could feel the calluses years of hard labor had left on his palms.

"Deputy sheriff. That can't be good."

"I'd just like to know if you can tell me where your son is."

"I suppose you're asking about James. He's the one who's always in trouble."

"Yes, sir. Do they call him Hitch?"

"I guess so. Those druggies he hangs around with. I still call him James. I saw him a couple days ago."

"Good. Do you know where I might find him?"

"Can't really say. Since he's become an addict, he moves around. He caught that terrible disease from me. Had a bad drinking problem when my kids were growing up. Been going to AA the last few years."

"How do you get in touch with James?"

"I don't. He stops by here out of the blue. Never know when he'll show up. He usually wants something."

"What did he want this time?"

"A check. He has his mail sent here."

"Any idea where I might find him?"

"Just an idea."

***

5 p.m.

"You guys mind working late tonight? I know it's already the end of your shifts, but I'd like to stay on this," Claire said. As chief investigator, it was just a gesture that she even asked them whether they minded. She was in charge.

Neither Amy nor Bill showed a lot of enthusiasm for the suggestion. They sat on either side of her, and both mumbled a disgruntled *no, they didn't mind and yes, they would work late.* They seemed to be trying awfully hard to ignore each other.

Claire was still wondering what was going on between the two of them. When she tried to ask Amy before, she had been evasive. When she got a chance, she'd ask her again. Either they really disliked each other or they were in love and trying to hide it. Maybe both.

Could make life interesting around the sheriff's office—fraternizing between deputies. Since Amy was only the second woman deputy in the department, there hadn't been much chance of a romance happening before.

The three of them were sitting around the conference table with their notes spread out. End of the day fatigue had set in. Each of them had a hand wrapped around a coffee cup. A half-pound Hershey bar lay on the table, cracked into segments, a few of which were missing.

Claire took a piece of chocolate and said, "Amy, why don't you start? Tell us what you got from Arlene and Jared."

"Not a lot that I hadn't guessed. Jared looks like shit, pardon my French. He's got all the signs of bad withdrawal from methamphetamine, very, very sleepy. His mom seems to know what's going on. He claims he's trying to quit. I threatened testing him for meth and he coughed up his dealer's name—Hitch. That's all he knew. This Hitch guy hung out at Letty's. I think if we find him we could at least get him for negligence in Letty's death. I'm sure he was behind the brew that blew up."

Bill nodded his head. "That's the name I got too. Nobody seems to know his real name, but they told me that a guy named Hitch was dealing meth in the area."

"Has he been on your radar?"

"No, I've been watching a dealer out of Eau Claire, who's been bringing stuff into the county. Hitch's not one of the big guys, he's not bringing stuff in from Mexico, which is where most of it is coming from now, but he's making it here. Just cooking up ounces, not pounds. No one I talked to seemed to know where he is right now. I don't think they were holding out on me."

Claire felt a little smug as she told them what she had found out. "I talked to Hitch's father."

Bill blurted out. "How'd you find out who his father is?"

"I talked to his brother."

Amy leaned forward. "What'd you get?"

"No one speaks too highly of him, except his dad. His brother has disowned him, claims he's responsible for his mother's death. Got her hooked on the stuff."

"No way," Amy said.

"The father says Hitch came over, looking for his social security check, which goes to his father's address."

"That crud is living off of social security. He should be shot just for that," Bill slammed the table with his hand.

"He told his dad that he was staying at a house outside of Fort St. Antoine. Down by the railroad tracks. Small, kinda cute. Gingerbread, painted light blue. You know the one?"

"That's a darling house. And I did hear it's rented out. Musta been to the wrong kind of people." Amy said.

Bill stood up. "I say we go visit him."

Claire grabbed his arm. "I say we sit down. So you sure you don't mind working a little late tonight?"

This time Amy and Bill were much more enthusiastic about working late.

"We want to do this absolutely right, by the book. We want this guy and we don't want to slip up in any way. Let's start writing up the search warrant. If we can catch Judge Habersham, we can grab Hitch tonight."

***

5 p.m.

Roger Jorgenson sat on his tractor on the edge of a corn field. He didn't seem to be able to think anymore. Or rather, he could only think about *one* thing. What had happened to his daughter?

He had just finished cutting the old corn stalks for fodder. He needed to do something concrete about finding out the truth about Krista's death.

He climbed down off the tractor without even brushing off his clothes, which were covered with chaff that flew off stalks, and got into his truck. He wouldn't tell Emily where he was going. It would just worry her.

Since Krista's death, Emily hardly seemed able to drag herself through the day. The doctor had prescribed some antidepressants. They did calm her down, but they also made her vague and very quiet. He hadn't realized how much he had counted on her for conversation. He knew he could be overbearing sometimes, but since Krista had died, it seemed like the stuffing had gone out of Emily. He even had to make dinner the other night.

He would drive to town and ask the sheriff what they were finding out about his daughter's death. He had a right to know. The squeaky wheel got the oil and he wanted to make sure they were staying on the case.

After the funeral, a few people had come forward and told him stories about someone they knew doing methamphetamines, but no one would tell him anything that seemed connected to Krista. Maybe the police knew more. Maybe they even knew who had given her the drugs.

Roger knew the road into town so well he could have driven it blindfolded. Only five miles and he was on Main Street. He drove up the hill to the county building and parked by the front door.

He had been to the sheriff's department once before when some kids smashed his mailbox with a baseball bat. A group of them would drive around and take turns hitting mailboxes. Lots of fun.

The sheriff had told him there was a rash of such incidents going around and that it was mighty hard to catch the kids who did it. Roger put up a new mailbox, just like the old metal one, but he put a big cement block in it and left it there for a couple months so if the kids tried it again, they would get a real surprise. It had never happened after that. He was kinda sorry.

After parking his car, he pushed open the doors and walked down a long hallway that led to the front counter. A woman clerk came up and asked him what he wanted. Roger didn't know her.

"I'd like to speak to the sheriff," he explained.

"The sheriff is gone for the day."

"Then can I talk to anyone who's working on the Krista Jorgenson case?"

She called to a young man who was walking out of the conference room. The man looked familiar to Roger. "Bill? Can you come up here?"

The deputy walked up and shook hands with Roger. "So sorry to hear about your daughter, sir. We're working hard on it. Hope to have something real soon."

Now Roger remembered. Bill had come out to the farm one year when he was a teenager and helped with the haying. Roger had been amazed at how hard he worked for a kid. When they were done, Roger gave him an extra five bucks.

"Hey, Bill. Thanks. This is just driving me crazy. Have you learned anything about what had happened? I was hoping after the funeral you might get some information."

"Sir, we've got some good leads. We're following them up right now and we'll let you know as soon as we can. Don't worry. We're going to get this guy."

"You know who he is?"

"We have a pretty good idea."

"Who?"

Bill glanced down, then said, "Let me walk you outside."

When they got outside, Roger turned to Bill and said, "Goddamnit, son. I'm her father."

"I understand." Bill looked around the parking lot. They were the only two people standing in the cold wind. "We'll have some news for you real soon. We got a lead on a meth house over to Fort St. Antoine, a rental. We'll let you know as soon as we know anything."

"In Fort St. Antoine?" Roger had a feeling he knew the house. There were only about a hundred houses in Fort St. Antoine and most of them had been in the same family for years. He knew one had been rented out recently.

"Yeah, that's it. I'll call you tomorrow."

Roger liked Bill and was sure he was a good deputy, but Roger wasn't going to wait for his call.

***

5:30 p.m.

When Meg walked into the house, Rich was sitting at the kitchen counter, reading the paper. Unlike her mother, he didn't ask her where she'd been. He didn't wonder why she was late. He didn't remind her that she was grounded.

Rich just looked up and smiled. He folded down the paper and asked, "How'd your day go?"

Meg didn't tell him that she had just walked all the way from Jared's house. She dropped her backpack off her shoulders and sat in a chair at the table and said, "Not bad."

"I'm glad to hear that. Your mom called. She's going to be late tonight and said we shouldn't wait for her for dinner. You want to go get a burger at the Fort? Play a little pool?"

"Naw. I got homework to do. I'll just make myself a sandwich. You go ahead though."

"You sure?"

"Yeah, I'll be fine." Rich liked to go down to the Fort and shoot pool and drink a beer or two.

"Okay. I won't be gone long."

"When is Mom coming home?"

"She wasn't sure."

Better and better. Meg couldn't believe her luck. Fifteen minutes later, Rich left, driving off in the old Honda Civic.

Meg took the keys to the truck which were hanging on a hook by the back door and held them in her hand.

Did she really want to do this? She needed to get Jared out of his house—where she could really grill him about what happened the night that Krista died. She understood that he didn't feel comfortable talking about it with his mother downstairs doing the laundry.

Even if her mom came home before Meg made it back, she would have a super good excuse. If she could tell her mother the name of the drug guy that had given Krista the meth, Meg didn't even care if she was grounded for a year. It would be worth it.

Maybe then her life would start to go back to what it had once been. Maybe she could talk to Curt again without feeling this huge lump of guilt rising up in her throat to choke her.

She called Jared's number before she left. His mother answered. "Hi, Mrs. Ecklund. This is Meg Watkins again. I forgot to tell Jared an important thing about that homework. It won't take a second. Could I talk to him?"

Jared came on the phone. "What?"

"I got the truck. I'll be there in about ten minutes. Why don't you try to get outside and meet me by the trees at the end of your driveway."

"Okay. I can do that. Thanks."

"Good. I'll see you."

The old Ford pickup was parked in the shadow of the barn. It still had a load of hay in the back that Rich used for bedding for the pheasants. Meg climbed into the truck. She had learned how to drive this truck on field roads, she should be able to manage it on the paved county roads.

When she turned the key in the starter, the engine chugged and whined. No one had driven the truck in a while. She tried it again, pumped the gas pedal a couple times, careful not to flood it. The engine caught in a roar.

CHAPTER 15

5:30 p.m.

When Roger got home, he found Emily stretched out on the couch with the newspaper on her lap. At first he thought she was sleeping. Then he saw she had a pencil in her hand. She was doing one of those Japanese number games. She said they calmed her down. Said she couldn't think of anything else when she was doing them. Sushi was the word that first came to his mind, but that wasn't right. Sudoku.

Roger had tried to work one of them, but all he ended up with was too many numbers in a bunch of boxes and nothing for sure. Sudoku was just plain frustrating.

"What do you want for dinner?" Emily asked as he stood in front of her. She didn't even bother to look up.

"I'm going out for a bit."

That got her attention. She lifted her head and he could see that she had been crying again. The ravages of tears turned her face red and left streaks on her cheeks. "But you just got home."

"I need a part for the tractor."

"At this time?"

"Emily, don't fuss."

She put down the paper. "Don't you dare tell me not to fuss. What's going on, Roger?"

"Nothing."

"Where did you go before?"

There was really no reason to lie about where he had been. "I went to the sheriff's office."

"Oh, Roger." She sat up and folded the paper. "Do they know anything? What did you find out?"

"Why do you think I found out anything?"

"I can see it on your face. Tell me."

"It's probably nothing."

"They know who gave Krista that horrible drug?"

"Not for sure. They've got some kind of lead. I don't know." He turned and tried to leave the room. "I'll be back in a while."

"I'm coming with you."

"To the hardware store?"

She stood up and grabbed his arm, holding it tight with her firm grip. "Don't even try to pull that on me, Roger. I know you better than that. If you're going to find this guy, I'm going with you."

"I can't stop you."

"That's right. Let me just tell Tammy that we'll be back in a while." She went upstairs to talk to their other daughter. Now, their only daughter.

Roger could hardly think of how hard this was on Tammy. She went up and down, crying, then so angry. He knew the feeling. She wanted to blame someone for what had happened to her sister. She wanted to get revenge. He did too.

Roger thought of leaving without Emily. The truck was parked right outside the house. He could be gone before she got downstairs. But then he decided that she deserved to be in on whatever happened.

This guy was going down one way or another.

***

6 p.m.

Jared managed to sneak out of the house when his mother was watching TV with Davy. In his stocking feet, he slipped out the side door and went around the back, then cut into the neighbor's yard, staying low until he made it to the trees. He tucked himself into the grove of cedar trees by the mailbox to wait for Meg.

He saw this old truck barreling down the road and stepped out of the trees. Meg rolled to a stop and he jumped in.

When he got into the cab with her, she sniffed. He wondered if he was still giving off the smell of meth. His mother had told him he smelled like vinegar. He knew what she was talking about although he had always thought the smell was ranker than that, more like battery acid.

Jared couldn't believe how out of shape he was. Even that short walk took it out of him. He slumped against the car door.

"You okay?" she asked, slowing down.

"Don't worry about me. Just get out of here." He waved at her to get going.

"Calm down."

Jared gave a snort. "I wish I could."

Meg put the truck in gear, drove down the hill and then pulled into an old cemetery. "Let's talk."

"This isn't far enough away."

"Your mom's not going to follow you. Even if she figures out you're gone."

"You don't understand."

"Tell me."

Jared didn't want to stay at the cemetery. He didn't want to stop for anything. He felt like shaking Meg. "I know a place to go where we'll be safe. It's a house not too far from here."

"Right here is fine for now. I want to know a few things before I take you any further." Meg touched his shoulder. "So tell me what happened to Krista."

He resigned himself to telling Meg something. "Where do you want me to start?" he asked.

"At the beginning."

"Have you ever done meth?" he asked.

"Are you wacko? No."

"Well, let me explain what it's like," he said.

Jared told her everything. Once he started, he couldn't stop himself. All the stories had built up inside of him for so long that it burst out. He'd had nothing to do for days but think about his life and what had happened. His mom didn't want to hear it. She just wanted him to get better. Whatever that meant.

He told Meg what it was like to take meth for the first time, how he had felt so strong and so on top of the world. The world shrunk and he grew and he never wanted to stop growing. His body encompassed the universe. He could do anything. He told her about that and she listened.

Then he told her how he started to do it once or twice a week, hoping to get back to that feeling, but it never quite happened again. How he needed to take a hit every couple days or he felt crushed. As if something was stepping on top of him, stomping him down.

She stared at him, but he didn't care. He wanted to explain, he wanted someone to know how it felt.

"Finally I couldn't live without it. Nothing else matters."

"Nothing else? Not even your friends? Like Krista? All I want to know is what happened to Krista that night."

"Just one of those things."

"What does that mean?"

"You know. Heard about the party and thought we'd see what was going on. When we got there, Krista was upset about something. She wanted to leave. She and I used to have a little thing a couple years ago. Before Curt. She said she wanted to go to the Maiden Rock. She always had a thing about that place. Special to her." Jared stopped talking, afraid he would say too much. His legs started jiggling and he rubbed the tops of them to calm down.

"I know that. Then what?"

"The usual. We parked. We had some beer. We were all drinking. Then we did some meth. She wanted to try it."

"I don't believe you."

Jared hated that Meg didn't believe him. It made him talk even more forceful about that night. "For real. We didn't make her do it. She was into it. She asked for it." Jared wanted to believe this, needed to believe it.

"Why didn't you stop her? You know what it's like, what it can do to people."

Jared shook his head. "She grabbed it away from me, then snorted some. I could tell it hit her hard. Man, she was flying." Even talking about it, reminded him of how good it could be, made him sweat for some.

"How do you know?"

"You could tell by looking at her eyes. Couldn't stand still. Started dancing around."

"Then what happened?"

Now Jared needed Meg to do what he wanted her to do. He had to get her to take him to Hitch. Even if Hitch wasn't there, the people who was staying with would probably have some meth.

"We need to go see him. Hitch. All I know is that the two of them ran off toward the Maiden Rock together." Jared put the hook in, "And Hitch came back alone."

***

6:15 p.m.

Amy and Bill walked over to a squad car and then both stopped about ten feet away from it. Amy knew that Bill liked to drive. She had told him that she thought they should trade off when they partnered together, but she wasn't sure he heard her, or liked the sound of that. Men could be so controlling.

"Is it your turn to drive?" Bill asked with a note of sarcasm.

He must have heard her. "Sure, I'll drive."

Bill still hesitated. "Do you think you'll be able to keep up with Claire?"

Claire was getting into the car parked next to theirs. She had said she wanted two cars at the scene, not knowing what they would encounter.

Amy snorted, and then was embarrassed that she had made such a geeky sound. "I could drive circles around her."

They got in the car. Amy followed Claire out of the parking lot.

"This isn't going to be fun," Bill said.

"I know that."

"Until you've done the real thing, you don't know."

There he went again, being so darn patronizing. She didn't know if he did it because he liked her or he just wanted to lord it over her. "Well, then obviously you can't tell me about it. I'll just have to go through it."

Bill looked out the window.

She wondered what he was thinking about. They had gone to the shooting range together last night, but it hadn't gone so well. Amy said, "I'm sorry if I'm a better shot than you are."

"I don't give a shit about that."

"Well, then why have you been so pissy around me since my score at the range was higher than yours?"

"If you want to know, I'm not unhappy about you having a better score. I just thought it was a little inconsiderate of you to brag about it so much."

Amy whooped.

Bill said, "Keep both hands on the wheel."

"All I did was tell Dirk that I hit the target twice as often as you."

"See, there you go again. If you want to know—deputy sheriffs don't do that. We don't brag about what we do right. It's our job. We just do it. I've shot much better than I did that day and kept it to myself. If you want to know the truth, I had kind of a hard time concentrating 'cause of you."

"You did?" Amy liked the sound of that. "Really?"

"Yeah. You squirm around so much."

That wasn't what she wanted to hear. Or maybe it was. "You know where we're going, don't you?"

"Yeah, but don't lose Claire."

"With you talking so much, I lost track of where we were."

They drove for a mile in silence. Amy was more excited than scared. She hadn't seen what she would call "action" since she had started working as a deputy.

"Let Claire and I go in first," Bill said.

"Why? You worried about me?"

"Seniority," Bill said, then added, "And I don't want you to get in the way."

CHAPTER 16

6:15 p.m.

Arlene kept her car at a distance behind the truck that Jared had climbed into. She didn't want to be seen. Not easy to do on country roads because there weren't any other cars to hide behind. When the truck stopped at the cemetery, she pulled in behind a grove of trees and waited. When the truck pulled out onto the road and went down the hill, she followed.

What she had most feared was coming to pass: Jared hooking up with one of his old cronies and getting back into that evil stuff. She would not let it happen again. She would put a stop to it once and for all. She would call the cops if she had to, but she hated to get them involved. Her son didn't need to go to jail; he just needed to get off that poisonous stuff.

Arlene had thought it was worth a try to see if she could help him get off the meth at home. Obviously that wasn't going to work when his source was so close at hand.

Davy sat in the back seat of the car, coloring in a book. His small head bobbed up and down with the movement of the car. She couldn't believe she was about to raise another child.

He looked up and asked, "Where's Mommy gone to?"

"Your mom is gone far, far away." A sadness come on her. She had hardly had time to mourn her sister's death. But then

Letty's demise had been going on for so long. Terrible to watch a woman waste away a day at a time for over five years now.

"Oh. She coming back?"

Davy hadn't asked much about his mother. He had become so used to staying at Arlene's house it had become a second home for him. Arlene didn't believe in heaven and didn't like to lie to children. "That's a hard question. I don't think so."

"She can come to your house. We live at your house."

"Why?"

"There's not so much icky smells."

Arlene had made an appointment with the doctor to check Davy out for exposure to chemicals. She wasn't looking forward to finding out how all that poison had affected the small boy. She hoped he had somehow avoided the worst of the contamination. He was such a good, quiet child. But that worried her too. Wasn't he too quiet? Shouldn't he have more energy?

Right now he was scribbling away at the coloring book, but often he just laid on the couch and watched TV.

He asked, "Where's Jared?"

"We're following him."

"How come?"

"To make sure he doesn't do something he shouldn't do."

"Oh."

***

6:20 p.m.

"That's his motorcycle," Jared said.

Meg saw the black motorcycle parked by the side of the gingerbread house and felt her muscles tightening across her chest. "Do you think he will really tell us what happened?"

"Why not? He doesn't care about stuff like that. I don't think he'll lie. Takes too much energy."

Even though Jared hadn't meant to be funny, Meg laughed. That was when she felt how scared she was. The tension bands around her body would hardly allow her to breathe.

They got out of the truck and she stuffed the truck keys deep in her pocket. The gingerbread house was small and ordinary-looking, painted a soft sage-green with white trim.

She noticed Jared was having trouble standing. He was shaking harder than he had in the truck.

"Are you okay?" She put out a hand to help him.

"Get out of my way," he said, jerking away and walking ahead of her.

She grabbed at him, but he pulled away again. "What're you going to do, Jared?"

He didn't say anything. When they got to the door, he banged on it harder than Meg would have believed he had the power to.

A voice from inside yelled, "Yah?"

"Hitch, it's me, Jared. You got any?"

Now Meg knew why Jared had wanted to come here.

She hadn't seen it coming. She thought she was using Jared to bring her to the dealer, when in fact he had been using her for the same purpose.

What would it be like to try that magic drug that made the world something you could hold in your hand while you flew away from it? What had Krista felt as she soared off the earth?

Why did Jared fight so hard to take it again? Meg wondered how it would make her feel.

The door opened. A gaunt old man stood looking out at them with big, bottomless eyes and a smile that was a black hole.

"Hitch, man, you got any stuff?" Jared asked.

But the thin man just stared past Jared at Meg. "What've we got here? Another lovely maiden?"

***

6:22 p.m.

As they drove down to Fort St. Antoine—heading toward a meth house, Roger said—Emily wondered how other mothers survived when their kids were killed. She felt as if she had joined a club she had never known existed before. Before she heard the words that told her Krista was dead.

Roger had his anger. It saved him.

Emily felt like all she had was her sorrow and it was endless. She was swimming in it and there was no shore in sight. She might never touch solid ground again. But she had to stay in the world. Her other daughter needed her. Roger needed her.

Never before had she known how much she had needed Krista.

***

6:30 p.m.

All he had wanted to do was finish brewing the batch. That's all.

But these people had to come knocking at the door, bugging him, asking him about the girl.

He didn't want to think about the girl. It wasn't his fault she couldn't handle the drug. He tried to tell them that. But they wouldn't listen.

There had been a fight.

When the knife went in him, Hitch thought that he had been kicked. Then he knew what had happened. He recognized the pain—thin and sweet.

He fell to the floor, his legs giving out. All he could see was the haze of the air. Another moment of life pulling away from him.

Out out out, buzzing around him.

The sky was falling on top of him and he couldn't push it away.

Just another trip, sliding out through the cracks. The knife had slit him open and his soul was winding its way out.

They were all gone. Everyone who had ever known him. All the people who had wanted everything from him. They were gone.

He wondered if his mother would be there to greet him. Please, let her be there, he prayed. Please let her forgive me.

Pain was his only company and he blinked it away.

Back.

Blink.

Back.

Done.

CHAPTER 17

6:45 p.m.

When Claire walked into the gingerbread house, she felt as if the witch was still living there. A deep foul smell made her gag and clap a hand to her mouth. What had the witch been brewing? She pulled a protective mask out of her pocket and slipped it over her head.

Two steps into the house and she could see the kitchen. Cupboards hanging open, every counter covered with crap.

Three steps in and she could see two jean-clad legs on the floor of the kitchen, in a pool of liquid. But it was not blood, not red.

The only noise she could hear was the hiss of the gas burner on the stove.

Four steps and she saw a skinny, dark-haired, unshaven man stretched out on the floor, a pot by his head and liquid all over the kitchen floor. Even through the mask, the stink was overwhelming. She knew she shouldn't even be in there. But she had to check on him.

Three more steps brought her to the body. Claire kicked his foot. Nothing.

She stepped up to his head, leaned over and put a finger to his neck. No pulse. Nothing stirred.

Reading the scene in front of her, it looked like he had fallen into the poisonous brew and drowned in it. Was that even possible?

Claire brought her eyes back to the skinny man. He was lying on his side, his feet stretched out straight. When she walked around him she saw the knife.

A knife stuck out of his back, right under his rib cage.

"Claire?" Bill yelled from outside the house. "You okay in there?"

"Yeah, come on in," she called.

Claire reached over the man and turned off the gas on the stove. The place was volatile enough on its own. Didn't need a spark from the stove to set the place off. She tried to open the window in the kitchen but found it was nailed shut. Paranoia.

"Prop the door open," she said. "And put on your masks."

Amy came in behind Bill. With their masks and their hats on it was hard to tell them apart. They both looked down at the body.

"Quite dead," Claire said.

"Good riddance," Bill said.

Amy snapped. "Don't even say that."

"He was a waste."

"He was a person."

"He quit being a person the first time he did meth, as far as I'm concerned," Bill said.

"He had a mother, a family. People loved him," Amy said.

"Doesn't sound like they loved him very much anymore. He was a loser," Bill argued.

"What do you know about it, you judgmental slob? My sister died from an overdose of cocaine. Nobody deserves to die like that."

That shut Bill up. He mumbled something that might have been, "sorry."

"You two need to focus," Claire said. "There's a knife in his back. I don't think he put it there himself."

"Why couldn't he have just died on his own?" Bill asked. "Then we wouldn't have to do anything."

Claire ignored his question although she had had the same thought. "Look around, try not to touch anything, and then let's get out of here. I don't want any of us in here for very long."

***

6:48 p.m.

Amy stared down at the meth dealer, the first dead person she had to deal with on her watch. Hitch's mouth was slightly open as if he were about to say something. His eyes stared into the farthest distance. His fingers were frozen into claws as if he had been trying to grab hold of the last bit of life.

It was less traumatic than she thought it would be. She was glad it wasn't a kid or a woman. That would be hard. But this skinny, scabby man looked like he had been aimed at death for a long time. A wave of sorrow came over her, remembering her sister. They hadn't even found her for three days after she overdosed.

The condition of the house was more shocking to her than the body. She had heard of such places, but couldn't believe people actually lived in them: the woman with forty cats, the man who never threw anything away, and now these meth users who fouled and trashed their own nest.

Amy carefully walked around the living room, looking for something that would tell them who had done this murder. How would she even know a clue if it was there—in among all the beer cans, newspapers, and fast-food bags?

Bill and Claire were going over the kitchen. Amy looked down the hallway and saw three rooms, two with closed doors. One she guessed was the bathroom, another the bedroom. Maybe she could get a window open in one of the rooms.

Amy pushed open the door of the bathroom, but didn't go in. The toilet wasn't working anymore, plugged up with toilet paper and excrement. The bathtub was filled with scummy water. The sink was not even visible under a pile of clothes and grungy towels. She left the door open.

She walked down the hallway and tried to open the other closed door. There seemed to be a slight resistance. She pushed harder.

The door flew open and she started to fall forward into the room.

A string ran from the door to a chair holding a shotgun.

First she felt the spray slam into her shoulder. Fire licked her cheeks, her shoulder and her arm.

Then she heard the slap of the shot that cracked the air.

CHAPTER 18

6:49 p.m.

Claire heard the shot, then a thud. Amy yelped, a short high cry that sounded like the noise a dog makes when it gets hit by a car.

Bill turned and ran toward the sounds. "Amy," he yelled. Claire was right behind him.

Amy had crumpled onto the floor in the doorway of a bedroom. Bill knelt next to her on the floor and checked her over. Blood gushed out of a hole in her arm and her face was smeared with red.

"I'm okay," Amy insisted as she tried to sit up, pushing his hands away. As she sat up her eyes rolled back in her head and she slouched forward in a faint. Bill caught her before she could fall.

"Where did she get hit?" Claire asked, looking back into the room at the shotgun that had blasted the deputy.

Bill was busy checking Amy's wounds. "It looks like the shoulder's the worst. She must have been turning away as she got hit only on one the side of the face. I can't find any bleeding on her torso."

"Thank god." Claire let Bill handle Amy as she put in an emergency call for an ambulance.

They managed to staunch the blood flow from the worst wound on her upper arm, but Amy came to and screamed, a horrible screeching sound that made Claire want to stop and cover her ears.

Bill put a very competent tourniquet at the top of the injured arm but the lacerations on her face and neck were still oozing blood. Unfortunately, by the time he got the tourniquet on, she had already lost a lot of blood. Claire hoped not too much.

When they settled Amy on the floor, she stopped screaming, but the occasional whimpers that escaped her lips were almost worse.

Claire whispered to Bill, "I'm worried about her going into shock. We've got to keep her warm."

Bill sat down on the floor and lifted Amy's head into his lap while Claire elevated Amy's feet on a cardboard box. He wrapped his jacket around the front of her body but Amy had already started to shake.

"Are you going to be okay? I want to see if the ambulance is coming," Claire asked.

Bill nodded and muttered. "Get out there and get them. She needs help."

Claire stood out by the highway for what felt like an hour but was only ten minutes. Then she went back in to the house to check on Amy and saw that the young deputy was, in fact, going into bad shock, probably stage 2 as they had called it in her last CPR class.

The young deputy seemed agitated and wasn't clear about who Bill was. She kept saying, "Don't shoot, don't shoot," and pushing his hands away as he tried to soothe her.

Claire knew that Amy's agitation and confusion were not good signs. They meant she needed oxygen, possibly even a blood transfusion.

Claire stuck her head back out the front door and was hugely relieved to see the ambulance pull into the driveway.

She ran up to the ambulance, yelling to the EMTs to go into the house, then decided to stay outside. They didn't need another person in that space; it was crowded enough as it was with two bodies stretched out on the floor.

Her phone rang. "Yeah."

Rich said her name.

"I can't talk now."

Rich spoke fast. "Claire, listen to me. Meg's gone. She took the old truck."

"What?" Claire leaned against the side of the ambulance. Why did Meg have to do this now when she had a badly injured deputy and a dead man to deal with?

"I went down to the Fort to grab a bite and when I came back she was gone. The truck is gone."

"How much gas was in that thing?"

"Enough."

"A note?"

"Nothing here on the kitchen counter. I haven't checked her room that thoroughly."

"You call Bridget?"

"Yeah, I called her. She hasn't heard from Meg."

Claire looked at the house. The EMTs were bringing a struggling Amy out of the house on a stretcher.

"I gotta go. We went into a meth house and Amy got shot up by a trap. I'm just about to call her parents." She decided not to mention the dead man—it would just take too long to explain. "Rich, can you find her? Can you just please find Meg?"

***

7:00 p.m.

Amy fought as hard as she could against the guards, but they were winning. She tried to get the man to help her, but he wouldn't. She knew his name was Bill. She was sure she knew him.

The guards were going to take her away. She didn't want them to hurt her anymore.

They had already clawed into her arm. She wasn't sure why they were doing this to her, but she had to fight them off.

Amy felt like she was going to throw up. Did they poison her?

Her face burned as if a cat had raked it with its claws. Her hand and arm were covered with blood. The man named Bill was trying to hold her hands, to quiet her.

She felt like he was on her side. "Why are they doing this to me?"

"You're going to be fine. They'll get you fixed up in no time," Bill said, but he wasn't looking at her face. He was just looking at her eyes.

"My face hurts."

Another voice said to her, "Ma'am, we need you to lie down." An arm pushed her back down on the stretcher.

"Are you coming with me?" Amy asked Bill.

"I'll be there soon."

"Don't leave me," she screamed as the guards put her into a prison wagon. The man wasn't coming with her. She was on her own. The guards were pushing her onto a bed and strapping her down.

Someone grabbed her arm and jabbed her with something. She screamed. No more. She couldn't take anymore pain.

Shivering wracked her body. They were trying to force something over her mouth so she couldn't breathe. She couldn't breathe.

"This is oxygen. You need it."

They were lying. Amy was sure they were lying. It was poison they were trying to force into her body.

She tried to push them away, but she couldn't even lift her arms. She felt so weak. The poison was flowing through her body.

She couldn't stop them.

She was dying. Faces stared down at her, then the world flashed black and vanished.

***

7:05 p.m.

Rich ran up the stairs to Meg's room. He stood outside her door for a moment, looking at the poster of a galloping horse she had pinned to her door. He had given her that poster for her twelfth birthday.

Sometimes he wished she was twelve again.

She had been so much easier to handle.

Meg had told him that she would stay home when he had left for the Fort. As far as he knew it was the first time she had ever lied to him.

Rich had checked her room when he was first looking for her, but hadn't really gone in and looked around. He pushed the door open and scanned the room to see if he could spot a note. Nothing. At least not in plain sight.

The covers of her bed had been tossed over it in what she claimed was "making the bed." Most of her clothes had been kicked into her closet, which left a small clear space in the middle of the floor. About once a month, Meg went on a rampage and cleaned her room. Then she let it get messy again. He wasn't sure what the tipping point was for her, when she couldn't stand it anymore.

Her desk was a pile of books and notebooks. Her laptop hummed but the screen was blank with a small light pulsing on the keyboard. As many times as Meg told him it was okay to let the computer run all the time, it went against his ways.

Rich decided to check her email. He hit the return key and the screen came to life. Hating himself for snooping, he clicked on her mail program.

When Meg's email folder opened, it made him sad to see that Krista's file was at the top of her screen. They had been such good friends. He knew how much Meg was missing her.

He checked Meg's messages. Nothing came in. The top message in her In-box was from Curt. The time line read from this morning. She hadn't answered it yet.

Rich clicked on Curt's message:

MEG,
JUST MOI. I KNOW U DON'T WANT ME TO WRITE U,
BUT I GOTTA. I HOPE U READ THIS. IF WE CLD JUST
TALK. NOTHING ELSE. ONLY U WLD UNDERSTAND.
THAT'S THE THING. LET'S MEET. ANYPLACE U WANT.
U MAKE THE RULES. YR BEST FRIEND, CURT

Rich wasn't sure what had gone down between her and Curt, but from the looks of the note, he might have been Meg's special someone. Rich had always liked the boy. Curt had an ease about him that was very genuine.

The few times Curt had come over he had seemed interested in the pheasants, asking questions that showed a depth of knowledge. When Rich asked him about his interest, Curt had explained, "I raised geese for 4-H a few years ago."

Rich had hoped that Meg could stay friends with Curt through all that had happened to the two of them, both of them being such good friends to Krista. But he knew enough not to say anything to Meg for fear she'd move in exactly the opposite direction.

So Meg might be at Curt's house. Or they could be meeting someplace. That made sense. Nothing to worry about. He just wished Meg would have let them know where she was going.

Sitting at Meg's desk, he picked up the phone, thinking to call Claire and tell her he was going to drive out to Curt's to see if Meg was there. Then Rich wondered if Meg had called someone after he had left for the Fort. Worth checking out. Claire had taught him how to do such things.

He pressed *69. The phone bleeped out a number and then it started to ring. Five rings, then a recording.

An older woman's voice said, "We're not here right now. Press 1 to leave a message for Arlene and 2 to leave a message for Jared. We'll get right back to you. Thanks for calling."

Rich hung up the phone without leaving a message.

Meg hadn't called Curt. Or at least, that hadn't been the last call she had made. Arlene and Jared. It sounded like she had called the Ecklunds?

Arlene and Jared Ecklund. Rich knew Arlene slightly. He was pretty sure that her son Jared was in school with Meg, but in a higher grade. He hadn't heard Meg mention him much. Rich didn't think they were particular friends or anything. But maybe Jared had been a friend of Krista's.

Then he remembered the conversation he had had with Meg when they came home from Krista's funeral. She said she knew someone at school that she should talk to about methamphetamine use. Could it be Jared?

Letty was Jared's aunt. It was a well-known fact that she was doing drugs. Maybe it had been meth. From the little he knew about that drug, people on meth had no scruples about getting loved ones hooked too.

CHAPTER 19

7:10 p.m.

Emily sat as still as a stone, leaning up against the car window as if she wanted to get as far away as she could from him. She didn't have her seat belt on. She wasn't saying anything.

Roger wasn't sure where he was going. He was headed south and thinking of crossing over into Minnesota at Wabasha. He just wanted to get away.

"What now?" Emily finally asked as he drove into Nelson.

"I don't know."

"We've got to do something," she said.

"What?"

"I don't know. Tell someone."

"What?"

"What happened."

"Why?"

"Because we're law-abiding citizens."

"Right," Roger said. "*We* play by the rules, but no one else has to. No one will believe us. That much is clear."

"That doesn't matter. We have to do it anyway. We can't just go driving all over the country."

Roger pulled over in front of the bar in Nelson and turned off the car. "I need a drink first."

"I could use one too." Emily opened the door, then looked back at him. "Then we have to go tell the sheriff."

"Okay."

"He's dead, you know. I'm sure he's dead."

"I don't doubt it." Roger put his arm behind his wife of twenty-three years and escorted her into a bar. Neither of them drank much and he was sure Emily had never been in this place before. He had only been in the bar once or twice in all his long years in this area.

The bar smelled of cigarettes and dung. Roger wasn't sure why it smelled that way, but he guessed maybe the farmers were tracking in manure on their boots. There were a couple older men up at the bar and a couple in the dark toward the back of the place.

"What would you like?" he asked Emily.

"I'll have whatever you're having. Something strong."

Roger ordered two Brandy Manhattans. The bartender poured generous shots into two highball glasses. "Anything else?"

"That's it." Roger paid, then grabbed the glasses.

The bartender tapped the fifty cent tip he had left him on the bar and said, "Have a good day."

Under his breath, Roger said, "Too late."

***

7:20 p.m.

The older clapboard house impressed Rich as tidy, but slightly shabby. He knew that Arlene's husband had died a few years ago. Rich had known her husband better than he knew Arlene. Bob

Ecklund had worked for the grainery in Durand. Rich often got his feed there. Bob had always struck him as a nice, steady guy.

He knocked on the front door, but there was no answer. He could hear voices inside. Maybe they hadn't heard him knocking. Most people probably used the side door. Most people probably just walked in.

Rich knocked again and then tried the door. It was not locked and opened easily. He stepped in.

The TV was on in the front room, but no one was watching it. He stood on the front door mat, a welcome sign with a cow on it, and hollered, "Anybody home?"

No answer.

Rich walked in and looked around.

In the kitchen it looked as if they had left in a hurry. A cup of coffee sat on the table, an open half-gallon milk container next to it. The inside side door to the kitchen was open. The screen door was shut, but not locked. There was no car in the garage or the driveway.

He didn't know what to think. He didn't know for sure that Meg had come over to Arlene's. Maybe she had called and no one had answered. Maybe she had dialed the wrong number.

But the state of the house bothered him. Arlene didn't strike him as the kind of person that would leave the TV on and the milk sitting out, even if she was just running next door.

Rich put the milk away and then walked into the living room and turned off the TV. The neighborly thing to do.

He would call Arlene later to make sure everything was all right.

Right now, he had to find Meg.

***

7:25 p.m.

When the Hazardous Materials team showed up, they pulled everyone out of the house and made them suit up. Several other squad cars showed up with more deputies, including Speedo—so named because of the quickness at which he could snap a photo. Claire followed the Haz-mat guys back into the crime scene, wearing a better mask and an orange coverall.

Hitch still lay sprawled on the kitchen floor.

Speedo squatted down next to Hitch's body, camera at the ready.

He looked up at Claire. "What do you want?"

"A couple close-ups of the knife, a couple full body, then from both sides. I'd also like you to take some pictures of the rest of the room; the whole house for that matter. It's all a crime scene."

He nodded at Hitch. "This is one emaciated dude."

Claire agreed. "He's been on a meth diet for too many years."

"I heard about Amy."

"Yeah."

"She going to be okay?"

"She took a load of shot." Claire didn't want to think about Amy. She had had to call Amy's parents and her mother had started crying before she could even say what had happened. They had moved down to Arkansas and wouldn't be able to get up to Wisconsin until tomorrow. Claire had assured her that Amy would be okay, didn't mention what her face had looked like. "You know what's going on about the medical examiner?"

"I think they had to call in some one from Eau Claire."

"Shit."

Since Dr. Lord had retired, they were often forced to use the medical examiner from Eau Claire. That meant it would be another hour or two before he got to Fort St. Antoine.

Claire walked into the bedroom to check on Bill. He was looking over the booby trap shotgun. "Nasty thing. How'd he know who'd open that door? Could have been a kid."

"His state of mind, he could have done it himself," Claire pointed out.

"I think Amy's going to be okay," he said it like it was a question.

"I hope so."

"Why did she get so nuts when they were taking her away?" Bill asked.

"Shock can do that to you."

"I'll stop by the hospital later tonight."

Once again Claire wondered what was going on between the two deputies. "That'd be great. Thanks, Bill. Have you checked out the other room?"

"No. Be careful."

"I'm nothing but careful."

Using a chair, Claire pushed open the door of the other bedroom. When nothing snapped at her, she reached in and turned on the overhead light.

A full-sized mattress on the floor with a Snoopy blanket mounded on it was the only piece of furniture in the room. There were no shades; the window had a flattened piece of cardboard nailed over it. Another sign of meth paranoia.

Other than the mattress, the room was stuffed with mail. Piles of mail carpeted the floor like a tidal wave, cresting at a foot or two high. Reaching down, she picked up an envelope.

Phone bill for a Mr. Anderson. She wondered if any of her mail was scattered on the floor.

Looking at the dark, mail-filled room Claire felt like she was seeing the inside of a methamphetamine user's brain. She had always had the theory that looking in people's houses was a lot like getting a peek into their psyches. What she saw in this room was an explosion of paper and words, a paranoia that knew no bounds.

Claire shivered and then tried to guesstimate how much mail was in the room. Two months worth of deliveries in Pepin County. How could this much mail be taken and not noticed to be missing? She looked down at another envelope. A Minneapolis address. That explained it.

She had heard of meth users supporting their habits by stealing identities. When they were high, they had infinite energy and an obsessive ability to focus. Going through mail and stealing numbers and selling them was a good way to use that energy and keep money coming in for their habit.

She hated to think of the work all this mail would entail. Looking at the piles, she thought of the manpower it would take just to sort through it all. She backed out and pulled the door shut. Another day.

Claire walked back into the living room to check on Speedo. He was snapping away. The house disgusted her. How could people live like this—the whole room was a garbage can, literally—beer cans, newspapers, rotten sandwiches, MacDonald bags, and worse.

There was a pile of something dark in the corner that she didn't even want to examine. She was glad to be wearing protection. Who knew what foul matter was in the air.

As she watched Speedo, she decided not to interrupt him. He seemed to be getting all the shots she wanted. Rich was always telling her she needed to learn to trust other people more. The house was stifling. She was sweating profusely in her orange overalls. She had to get out of the house for a moment, breathe some real air.

As Claire pushed open the screen door, something glinted on the floor and caught her eye.

She leaned down and picked up a friendship bracelet with red and blue beads braided into it. It looked like the strings had frayed and broken. She examined it more closely.

Her heart stopped.

She had seen this bracelet before. It was Meg's. Small white beads spelled out her first name.

Meg never took it off, not even when she showered.

Krista had made the friendship bracelet for Meg's birthday.

CHAPTER 20

7:25 p.m.

Head down, Meg pushed a path through a field filled with flower skeletons. That's the way they looked to her. Brown skeletons of dried-up goldenrod and coneflower.

A cold wind rattled the grass. Clouds scudded across the dark sky. The half moon was in the western sky, giving off a thin light.

She didn't know where Jared had gone. She didn't care anymore. She kept her hand wrapped around what she had grabbed away from him before she had jumped in the truck and drove off. Why had she done that? Should she have left him there? What good would staying have done?

Everything seemed completely hopeless to her. Despite her best intentions, actions of hers had resulted in death. She should just learn that nothing she did made any difference.

She wished she could talk to Krista about what was going on. Krista would tell her what to do. Krista had always had an opinion about everything and never hesitated to give it. Or Curt. She needed someone on her side. Someone who would understand what she had done.

She had known Krista since fifth grade when they were in classes next door to each other. That was before they became best friends. She remembered so clearly how their friendship had started. Sarah Larsen had been standing in the hall talking in a really loud voice about how stupid the movie *Brokeback Mountain* was. Krista had been getting into her locker and Meg had been arguing with Sarah about the movie, which she had loved.

Sarah said, "The only people who could like that movie are liberals and homosexuals."

Krista had slung her arm around Meg's neck and kissed her under the ear in a very seductive manner. Then she had turned and said to Sarah, whose mouth was hanging open, "We're both."

Meg had been both shocked by and adoring of what Krista had done and wished she had thought of it.

That was at the end of eighth grade and they had been best friends this whole last year. Until Halloween.

If only there was no such thing as methamphetamines in the whole wide world.

Meg had known that methamphetamines were being used in this area. A month or two didn't go by without the school bringing some kind of speaker—an ex-druggy, a rehab counselor, a concerned mother—to talk to the students about how bad drugs were for you. Meg had always thought the talks were stupid and over the top. She had never had the impulse to try a drug particularly, but she didn't believe they could totally destroy your life the way these speakers said.

Now she believed it all. She had seen it with her own eyes. The ravaged body of Hitch, the foulness of the nest he lived in, the stench of the drug he was concocting, she would never forget any of it.

Meg knew she would have nightmares about Hitch. Jared didn't look so good, but Jared mainly just looked skinny and wasted. She didn't know how Hitch could still be alive. His face was pockmarked. He had few teeth left in his mouth. His breath was noxious. His eyes were sunken into his skull. He looked like the soul had been sucked out of him and all that was left was a few bones and tendons. No mind, no muscle, no spirit.

She wondered what Hitch had been like at her age, if he had played a sport, if he had thought of going to college, if he had had a girlfriend. Hard to imagine a normal life for him as he had truly become a monster.

She didn't know how badly she had hurt him. She didn't care. She hoped, for everyone's sake including his own, that Hitch was dead.

She kept walking. The Maiden Rock was on the other side of the skeleton-littered field, past the trees.

Meg looked down at the square of tinfoil she was holding in her hands.

Methamphetamine.

What would it be like to try a little? Just to know what Krista had felt before she left the earth.

***

7:25 p.m.

"Where we going?" Davy asked, poking a finger at Jared.

Jared was sitting next to Davy in his car seat and he had his feet stretched out under the driver's seat, but he felt totally cramped. He had been trying to sleep, but for the first time since he had come off meth, he wasn't tired.

Davy poked him again.

He poked Davy back. "I don't got a clue."

"You don't gotta clue?"

"No clue," Jared repeated.

Davy held up two fingers. "This is two."

"How old are you?" Jared asked him.

Holding down his thumb and his pinkie finger, Davy managed to get three fingers sticking up. "I'm this many. I'm free."

Jared had no idea where his mother was taking him or even what she was thinking. When he had been outside Hitch's place, trying to figure out what to do after Meg took off, she had pulled up in her car. She grabbed Jared by the arm, and ushered him into the backseat. Without saying a word, she drove away. Jared hadn't even tried to stop her.

His mom had locked the back doors, child safety feature on this car, but he didn't care. He didn't care what happened to him anymore.

His Nikes were sitting on the seat next to him.

He put them on and didn't ask anything.

She was driving north on Highway 35. Not in the direction of their house. In fact, they were pretty close to Prescott. Maybe they were going to the cities. Maybe the Mall of America. But she drove through Prescott and kept going north. They were now heading toward Hudson, but he couldn't figure out why.

He sat up. "Where we going?"

"You'll see."

"Mom, tell me."

"A place I should have taken you long ago. You're done with that meth stuff for the rest of your life."

Meth, even the word made his heart race and his muscles tighten.

Somehow he had gone to see Hitch and left without any meth. A minor miracle. Or a major disaster. He wasn't sure anymore.

All because of Meg. She had taken him there and then she had saved him from it.

He hoped she was okay.

***

7:30 p.m.

Rich tried to call Claire on her cell phone, but got no answer. Then, on the way to Curt's house, Rich saw all the squad cars lined up along Highway 35. He pulled over and sat in his car, wondering if he should go talk to her.

An orange-suited person walked out of the house and Rich recognized Claire when she pulled off a full-face mask.

He got out of the car. She looked over at him and waved.

He could see the pressure marks from her face mask circling her eyes and mouth. Sweat beaded on her skin. Her eyes were wide open and her forehead wrinkled, deep lines between her eyebrows. Claire looked more anxious than he had seen her since Meg had disappeared. And now her daughter was gone again.

"What's going on in there?" he asked.

"God, you don't want to see it. Unbelievable. The pure squalor. I don't understand how people can keep living as long as they do when they abuse themselves so much. But he's dead now."

"Who?"

"This dealer named Hitch. It's been a nightmare. He had set up a shotgun trap and Amy opened the door and got hit by it."

"She going to be all right?"

"If she's not, I'll kill him again." Claire was silent for a moment, then she spit out, "Fucked-up paranoid son of a bitch's dead. Good riddance."

Rich listened to her swear. She didn't do it often, even though he knew it was not uncommon language with the deputies, so when she did the words hit him hard. "Sounds like it."

"His full name was James Hitchcock. You know him?"

"Just heard of his brother, like I told you." Rich watched Claire. "What happened? Overdose?"

"No, he got help. A knife in the back. I hope it was some deal gone bad."

He could tell from her face that she wasn't telling him something. "What else could it be?"

"Well, we think he might have been the guy who gave Krista the meth."

"And?"

Claire looked up at him, worried. "What if someone else found that out? Someone who loved Krista?"

"Like who?"

"Oh, Rich."

She grabbed his hand and leaned into him, avoiding looking at him. He didn't like this. "What?"

"I picked this up in this house, on the floor right by the door." She opened her hand and showed him Meg's friendship bracelet.

"Shit."

"I know."

"Aren't you supposed to have that in an evidence bag?"

"If it's evidence," she said quietly.

"What're you going to do with it?"

She jingled the bracelet in her hand, then tucked it away in her pocket. "I don't know."

CHAPTER 21

7:35 p.m.

Rich left, telling her he was going to talk to Curt, assuring her that he would find Meg wherever she was. Claire couldn't stand the thought that her daughter had been to see Hitch, that she was mixed up in this mess in any way.

After checking on Speedo again, she told the other deputies that she was going to talk to the neighbors. Mr. Bagley lived across the street. She didn't know him well even though she had lived near him for years. A widower, he kept to himself. While he was probably in his late eighties, his house and yard were always immaculate.

Looking down the street, she could see him in his yard on his riding lawn mower, studiously minding his own business despite all the cop cars.

She pulled off her orange suit and dropped it and the mask in the back of the Hazardous Materials truck.

It was getting dark out and her daughter was missing again. If only Claire had been there for dinner tonight, if only Rich hadn't gone to the Fort—but they couldn't watch Meg all the time. She was fifteen years old. Around the world girls were getting married off at that age, having babies.

Claire allowed her mind to slip into a place she didn't want it to venture: what if Meg had had something to do with Hitch's death?

She knew how devastated Meg had been by Krista's death. But she had to keep reminding herself that Meg didn't believe in killing—not anything. Her daughter walked wasps out the door on Kleenex, rather than squash them. If a bat flew into the house, she opened all the doors and windows until it found its way out again.

When they had first moved in with Rich, Meg had explained, "No need to hit it with a tennis racket. We're on the same side. We want the bat out. The bat wants out. All we need to do is help."

As Claire approached Mr. Bagley's house, he was riding his lawn mower into the garage. She yelled to him to let him know she was there so she wouldn't startle him. He was wearing a John Deere baseball cap with wisps of white hair sticking out behind his ears, and clean jean overalls over a plaid shirt.

When he saw Claire, he got off his mower and walked over. "Hopefully the last time I'll have to mow this year. Put it to bed, I say. Not often that I mow in November. Still pretty warm for this time of year."

"That'll change."

"You can count on it." He wiped his hands on his overalls. "What's going on over there?"

"I'm Claire Watkins, a deputy with the sheriff's department."

"I know who you are. It's about time."

"What's about time?"

"For someone to check on that house."

"Did you call the sheriff?"

"I was getting ready too. I try to mind my own business, but there's no good going on there."

"Like what?"

"Too many cars. Lights on all night long. People coming and going at every which hour. I've had my suspicions."

Claire understood Mr. Bagley's hesitance to report on a neighbor, but she didn't want to argue about that. "Well, you were very observant, Mr. Bagley. Have you been watching that house today?"

"Can't help but see it. It's right out my kitchen window. Where I eat dinner and watch my little TV I got set up on the counter."

"Can you tell me what went on there today?"

"Sure, come on in the house and I'll show you my view." Mr. Bagley turned and walked up the back steps into the house.

Inside his small house was as neat and tidy as outside. The living room was immaculate with a couch and two chairs. A print of Jesus praying with his hands coupled together hung over the couch. Claire followed him through into the kitchen.

This appeared to be the room where he spent most of his time. A small television set was sitting right under the cupboards. Mr. Bagley could sit at his formica table and watch TV and look out the window at the same time. He had a clear view of the gingerbread house.

"You know, they're renters. That's part of the problem. Renters never care about anything. They don't mow the lawn, they don't water. They figure it's not their problem. I've tried to stay out of their way. To tell you the truth, I'm a little afraid of that bunch, motorcycles and all."

"So who actually lives there?"

"That's a good question. A woman from California bought the house. She stayed there this summer and fixed it up. Nice lady. Then she left and rented it out to some woman. That's when all the problems started. I don't know if that woman is even there anymore. People come and go. I try to stay out of their way. But I've had a suspicion that they're selling those drugs over there."

"I'm afraid you're right."

"You don't say."

"So tell me who all was there today, please."

"Well, this real skinny guy's been staying there the last week or so. He rides that motorcycle. Geez, I hate those things. Don't they need to have mufflers on them? They're so loud."

"Okay, I know who you mean. That would probably be James Hitchcock."

"What is he some kinda outlaw or something? Anyway, today it's been kinda quiet over there until late afternoon, this old Ford pickup truck pulled up. A young girl was driving. Didn't even look old enough to drive."

"Dark hair?"

"Yeah, you know her?"

"I think so. Go on."

"And some skinny kid got out of the truck too. They went in to the house, then the girl came out, followed by the boy. They argued. After that the girl left. Alone."

"They argued?"

"Yeah, the girl talked to the kid, grabbed something away from him, then she started running and jumped into the truck and tore away. The kid came after her, but she didn't even slow down."

"Can you describe the boy?" Claire wondered who had been with Meg. It could have been Curt, or Jared. Rich said that Meg had called Jared before she left the house in the truck.

"Dark hair. I'd say about six feet tall. Real thin. Oh, and the funny thing, he wasn't wearing any shoes."

"No shoes? A little too cold to be going barefoot."

"He wasn't barefoot either. He had on socks."

"But she left him there?"

"Yeah, then almost immediately another car showed up. A woman about your age got out, grabbed the boy, pushed him in the backseat of her car and drove off."

"What did this woman look like?"

"Dark hair, stocky, about your age."

Claire supposed the woman could have been Jared's mother, Arlene. "Was that it?"

"Nope. About fifteen minutes later a fairly new Buick drove up—a farmer's car if there ever was one. A couple got out of the car. A man and a woman. I don't know what they were doing there. Seemed like nice normal people. They went into the house. Weren't in there very long and they came out again. It looked to me like the woman was hunched over, crying. Couldn't be sure. They turned around and drove back toward Nelson, heading south."

Claire didn't have a clue who that could have been. Then she remembered the car that the Jorgesons had driven to the funeral. A burgundy Buick. "Do you remember what color it was?"

"Dark. Could have been maroon, could have been navy."

"That's it?"

"No, then you." Mr. Bagley rested both his arms on the table. "Now, I want to ask you a question. What the hell's going on over there?"

"You were right. Looks like they were small-time dealers. They were only making enough meth for themselves and to sell on the side. Not that that makes it any less illegal and toxic."

"I hope you throw them all in jail."

"Well, James Hitchcock, the dealer, is dead. He was alone in the house when we got there. It looks like someone killed him."

"Someone killed him today?"

"Yeah, I'm afraid so."

"One of the people I saw."

"Most likely."

"You'll find out who did it?"

"Yes, I'm sure we will."

Mr. Bagley stood. "I'm sorry it's come to that. A death and all. I should have said something sooner. That's a bad place. You need to shut that place down and burn it. Good for nothing."

***

7:35 p.m.

Roger counted the cherry stems. Six of them. They had each had three Brandy Manhattans. More alcohol than they usually drank in a month.

"We've had a good marriage," he said to Emily.

"Better than most," Emily agreed.

"Whatever happens, I'll take care of everything."

"You're a good husband."

Emily was cute when she got drunk. She smiled a lot and stuck her finger in her drink and poked at the ice cubes. She had insisted on eating all the Maraschino cherries.

They hadn't talked about what they saw at the meth house. They hadn't talked about Krista. They really hadn't talked much at all. Just enjoyed their Brandy Manhattans.

Roger felt the urge to reach out and hold Emily's hand, but he didn't. He was afraid she would break down if he touched her.

They had loved each other for a long time. Since she had been a junior in high school and he was a senior. They had married as soon as Emily had graduated. But it took them almost ten years to get her pregnant the first time. Krista had been born two days after their tenth anniversary.

Roger had felt as if his heart would burst when he saw Krista in his wife's arms for the first time. A patch of red blond hair sprouted from the top of the baby's head. He had promised himself then and there that he would protect them with his life and somehow he had failed.

Then seven years later, along came Tammy. And his heart grew big enough to love all three of his girls.

Now, he had to protect Emily and Tammy from what had happened to them.

Emily drank the last swallow of her brandy. "Roger, I suppose we should get on with it."

"Yeah."

She looked over at him. "You know we might get lucky and get arrested for drunk driving. Then they could drive us to jail."

"There's one more place I want to go before we go to the sheriff's," Roger said.

***

7:50 p.m.

When she got back to the gingerbread house, Claire saw that a white Toyota Corolla was pulled up behind her squad car. She wondered if it belonged to a reporter, or maybe someone in forensics.

Claire wiggled her way back into her suit and pulled her mask on. When she went back into the house, she saw someone bent over Hitch's body. It was hard to tell who everyone was with all the orange they were wearing and the face masks. Even people she knew she didn't recognize.

She introduced herself and heard a thin, sharp voice say, "I'm Dr. Whitaker."

Resisting the urge to say it's about time, Claire asked how it was going. Dr. Whitaker didn't look up, just replied. "Why don't you let me finish up in here and we can talk outside. This is a hell of a place to be working in. I want to remove the body as quickly as possible."

Claire couldn't agree more. She went through the house and checked on all her deputies. She'd let them gather stuff for another hour or so, then shut the house down for the night.

The crime scene photos were done. Speedo had already left to print them. The kitchen and the living room had been dusted and fingerprinted. Charlie said they got so many prints, the whole county of Pepin had probably come through this place. Claire called for another ambulance to remove the body and take it to the morgue. Be ready to roll when this Whitaker was done. Must be a new guy. She hadn't heard of him before. Claire hoped he was good.

Looking over at the doctor, Claire saw him motion to go outside. She followed him out the door and they both walked a few yards away before lifting their masks. Dr. Whitaker revealed lovely blue eyes when she took off her face mask and then long, blond hair when she pushed back her hood.

"You're a woman." As soon as the words were out of her mouth, Claire wished she could pull them back.

"Yup, I bet you get that all the time too."

"Not as much as when I first started. It's been over eight years now." Claire looked at the short, stocky woman. "What can you tell me?"

"Not much that you don't know. I'd say he died in the last few hours. No rigor at all yet. Body temp still close to normal. Has a nasty hematoma on the back of his head, but I don't think that killed him. I'd have to guess it's the knife. Must have gone right into the liver. Someone knew what they were doing."

Claire thought, it wasn't Meg. She would have probably slashed at his hands or face, just to defend herself. "Have you taken the knife out yet?"

"No, I want to get him into the morgue and then I'll do the full autopsy."

"Can you get to that tonight?"

"I don't have a big date or anything if that's what you're asking. Might as well take care of it as long as I'm here."

CHAPTER 22

8:00 p.m.

Jared sat in a green chair. The woman behind the desk looked like a librarian. She had on glasses and had her grey-streaked hair pulled back in a bun. She told him her name was Libby Lowell.

She looked over her notes and then asked, "Jared, can you tell me when was the last time you used?"

"What do you mean?"

"What's your drug of choice?"

"Meth."

"When was the last time you used meth?"

"Almost a week ago, I guess."

"Good for you."

"My mom locked me up. I didn't have a choice."

The woman didn't say anything for a moment, then asked, "What other drugs have you been using?"

"I have a drink once in a while. I've taken some downers to get some sleep. But it's pretty much just meth."

She looked over her notes a while longer, then stood up and took the chair next to him. Jared wondered what the psychology of that was, getting closer to him, on more equal terms.

Libby took off her glasses and her eyes bore into him like nails. "Are you ready to do this?"

"Do what?"

"Go into treatment."

"I don't know."

"You need to decide. Just being here is already a decision."

"My mom made me come."

"What do you want to do?"

Jared thought about it. If he walked out of this room now, his mom would be waiting and she would freak out. She might give up on him. He'd be on his own. He would start taking meth again, which made his whole body tense just to think of it, but he'd have no home, no money. He'd die. Like Krista. The meth would kill him this time. He knew it.

"I guess I'll stay. What do you do here?"

Her lips turned up. A tight, serious smile. "Do you know anything about the twelve steps?"

"That's for alcoholics, isn't it?"

"Not just for them."

"How long will I be here?"

"That all depends on how your recovery proceeds. We will evaluate you the next couple days and make out a plan for you, which will be reevaluated several times while you are here."

"What if I did something really bad while I was using?"

"What do you mean?"

"What if I, like, did something really bad, stole something?" He thought about Krista. "Or even worse?"

***

8:00 p.m.

The cows strolled in from the pasture as Curt looked out of the barn—Greta, Hilda, Laura, Polly, Ellie. Large beautiful Guernseys. He had always thought they had such soulful eyes, outlined in dark, splots of brown mottled over their cream coats. They came in a line and headed to the barn. They knew the way.

When Curt turned, he saw his father was getting ready to hook the cows up to the milking machines. He inhaled deeply, loving the scent of a dairy barn, sweet milk, hay and manure.

As he walked over to help, he saw a dark-haired man standing in the doorway of the barn.

His dad noticed him, too, and walked over. "What can I do for you?"

Curt stopped and listened.

"I'm Rich Haggard. I think we've met at the Co-op."

"Sure, Rich, what can I help you with?"

"Actually it's your son I'd like to talk to. He's a friend of Meg's—Meg Watkins—my kindof stepdaughter." Curt knew and liked Rich. He hadn't recognized him at first. He always remembered how Meg had described him before Curt had met him, "part Clint Eastwood, part Al Gore, all pheasant farmer."

"Meg went for a drive a few hours ago and hasn't come back. I wondered if Curt might know where she could have gone."

"Curt," his father hollered.

Curt stepped forward and shook Rich Haggard's hand. He felt Rich's hand tighten and then release, as if he was testing Curt's strength.

"Mr. Haggard, nice to see you again. I heard you say Meg's missing."

"Yeah, as you know she's been grounded."

Curt's father went back to work.

Curt looked down at the barn floor and kicked at it with his boots. He had been luckier than Meg in that regard. His mother knew, but his dad never found out. He had slipped in to his bedroom safely. Even later, when they had all talked about Krista's death, he had never let on that he had been gone the whole night. They had felt so sorry for him, that his girlfriend had died, that his parents had let him be.

"Sorry about that, sir. I didn't mean to get her in any trouble. We didn't do anything. We were just talking." He hoped his father wasn't listening. Not that it would matter much, but he just didn't want to have to explain.

"Well, she's gone missing. She took our old truck and has been gone for a couple hours. Not a note, no nothing. I wondered if you might know where she went, if she had said anything to you."

"I'm the last person on earth who would know where she is. She won't even talk to me."

"Why?"

"I guess because of what happened to Krista. Somehow she's decided it was all our fault."

"I knew she'd been blaming herself. I didn't know she was blaming you, too." Rich rubbed the toe of his boot in the barn dirt. "I haven't tried to talk her out of that idea yet. I've figured she'd come around. She's a pretty level-headed kid."

"Yes, she is. She's very level-headed."

"If you hear from her or think of any place she might be, give us a call. I'd appreciate it."

"I'll do that, sir."

Curt watched the man leave the barn, then got back to work. He leaned his head against Donna, his favorite cow, and hooked her up to the milking machine. Her warmth reminded him of leaning into Meg's hair. She would hate him to tell her that. Meg. He missed her all the time. How was he ever going to get her back?

Curt looked out the barn door, saw the half moon sailing in the sky. Where would she go?

Suddenly it struck him clear through his body. The moon. The best view of it in the county. He was pretty sure he knew where to find Meg.

***

8:00 p.m.

Amy felt as if she was floating on an inner tube going down the Rush River. She was cold and groggy. She forced herself to open her eyes and found she was in a dimly lit room with someone sitting near her.

"Who're you?" she asked.

The man leaned forward and touched her hand.

She flinched.

"Amy, it's me, Bill."

"Bill, like deputy Bill." That struck her so funny that she started to laugh, which hurt, and then she started to cough, which really hurt.

"You want some water?" he asked.

"Please."

He poured her a glass from a plastic pitcher that was sitting on a rolling table next to her bed. "Where am I?"

He handed her the glass of water, positioning the straw, not letting go of it when she had it, treating her like she was an invalid. "Hospital. Do you remember what happened?"

She tried to put the glass to her face, but she couldn't seem to find her mouth and the water dribbled down her front. Bill helped her and she managed to swallow a little. "Not really. I was getting chased by mice or rats or cats or something. Wait, didn't we go into a house?"

"Yes and you got shot by a trap the dealer guy had set."

"Why are you here?"

"We finished at the house for the night. Claire shut down the crime scene. They took the body away and so I stopped by."

"Whoa, what body?"

"The dealer."

"He died?"

"He got killed."

"Who killed him?"

"That's the question."

Amy struggled to sit up. Her arm ached and her face hurt. Her left arm was bandaged, as was her left hand. Her right arm and hand looked all right. She put her right hand to her face. "Oh, God, what happened to my face?"

"You took a few pellets there, but they just grazed you. You don't look too bad."

"Now I'm really scared. What do you mean pellets? Did I get in a fight? Turn on the light."

"Are you sure?"

"Bill, what are you doing here?"

"I just wanted to make sure you were okay."

The way he said it she knew that recently she hadn't been okay. Her head hurt way deep down inside.

Bill reached over and turned on the fluorescent light above the bed. Amy looked down and saw she was in one of those completely unattractive sack-like hospital gowns and tucked into white sheets. The look on Bill's face told her how bad it had been.

She was starting to remember things, a dream worse than any she had ever had before. "What the hell happened to me?"

CHAPTER 23

8:30 p.m.

Meg sat on the edge of the Maiden Rock, the limestone gritty beneath her jeans. She had unwrapped the tinfoil package and was staring at the meth. The drug looked just like about a teaspoonful of baking powder. Such an insignificant substance and yet it had destroyed her best friend. Blew her off the face of the earth.

The scene at the gingerbread house had stunned her, too.

When Meg had walked into the house and seen the way Hitch was living, the way he looked at her, she wanted to be no part of it. If Jared wanted to kill himself with that poison, she was leaving. So she turned to go. Before she could get away, Hitch grabbed her hair.

Without thinking, she braided her fingers together into one huge fist, swung around as hard and fast as she could, and slammed her doubled fist into his head.

He went down hard. Meg ran out of the house.

Jared came out behind her, asking her to wait. He tried to talk to her, holding the hit of meth in his hands, saying he just needed this last little taste and then he'd be okay. If she would just wait for him and they could leave together. Maybe he could get back home before his mom even knew he was gone.

She was sick of Jared and his crap. He was nothing but a damaged soul. She felt like walloping him too.

Instead she grabbed the hit of meth out of his hands and ran to the truck.

He chased after her, but he was much too slow. She drove off before he even got to the back of the truck. He could figure out how to get home on his own, or he could go back into that putrid house and suck up all the meth his little brain could handle. She didn't care anymore.

All she had wanted to know was what had happened to Krista. When she had asked Hitch about that, he had dodged the question. But even if Hitch could remember what had happened—which she doubted—he wouldn't be able to coherently tell her. And Meg was coming to see that what she really wanted to know was how Krista had felt as she had flown away.

Sitting on the edge of the Maiden Rock, Meg also thought about the Indian maiden Winona.

What had Winona been thinking when she jumped off the bluff?

Krista had always been a little obsessed with the story of Winona and the Maiden Rock. Winona's father, Wapasha, was forcing her to marry an old warrior named Red Wing instead of the young brave that she loved. Some versions of the legend have her jumping to her death alone, some have her and the Indian brave leaping off the bluff edge together.

The way Meg saw it, either way she died.

Krista had thought the story was so romantic.

Meg thought their deaths had been a waste. Old Red Wing would have died soon enough. Why couldn't the two of them just have waited it out? Then they could have gotten married and lived happily ever after.

Meg thought about the collision of the Maiden Rock legend and what had happened to Krista and saw some weird parallels. Meg had taken Curt—her young beloved brave—away from Krista, and the old meth dealer who may as well been named Red Wing had stepped in, offering her a drug. She took it and jumped off the cliff.

This meant that Krista's death was all Meg's fault.

The half moon shone off the lake. The lake slithered down through the bluffs, right under her feet.

Meg touched the powdered meth in her hands. All she had to do was lower her head and breathe in. Breathe in.

***

8:30 p.m.

Amy stared at the hospital food on her dinner tray. Because of her loss of blood, they were forcing liquids into her: chicken broth, chocolate milk, ruby red jello.

She picked up the chocolate milk and took a sip. Then she looked up at Bill. "I'm hungry. Are you hungry?"

"I'm always hungry."

She offered him her jello.

"No, thanks. I don't eat red food. Especially anything that wiggles."

Amy knew he had to be starving. It was way past dinner time. "Why don't you go get us some real food?"

"What would you like?"

Normally, Amy tried to watch what she ate and lived on yogurt and salads and fruit, but she was really hungry. "I think I want a hamburger."

"Can do. What on it?"

"Everything."

"I'll be back."

As soon as Bill left, Amy felt herself give in to the painkillers. She stretched back on the bed and fell asleep.

About a half an hour later she woke up. Someone had come and taken her tray of food away while she slept. She had to pee. She was sure she could manage it herself. She slid her feet off the bed and pushed herself up with her good arm. The room spun but then righted itself.

Slowly Amy shuffled forward, holding onto the bed, then the wall until she came to the bathroom door. She pushed it open, didn't even bother to turn the light on, and sat on the toilet. After mission accomplished, she stood in front of the sink to wash her hands and turned on the light.

A monstrosity looked back at her from the mirror. A slash and a gouge dug into her cheeks with black stitches holding them together, bruises already discoloring her face. Her neck was bandaged and her lips were bruised and puffed out.

She had never considered herself a beauty, but she had always liked the way she looked—wholesome and cute. There would be no covering the scars that she would have on her cheek from the bullet holes.

She was hideous. Amy slid down to the tile floor. Tears streamed down her face.

"Delivery boy," Bill called from the next room.

She heard herself sobbing. She didn't seem to be able to rein herself in. The tears came harder. She didn't want Bill to see her like this.

"Amy?"

"Go away," she managed to spit out.

She was crying so hard she couldn't see to get up. The door pushed against her and Bill's face poked in. "What're you doing down there?"

"Get out of here." She bent her head and sobbed.

"Don't you feel good?"

"No." Between gasping, wrenching sobs, she managed to stutter out, "I look like a slasher victim."

Bill squeezed into the bathroom with her and put his arms around her. "You look like you've been hurt. That's all. You look like a deputy shot in the line of duty. Very honorable. Within a few days, you'll look better. Let's get you back in bed."

"Don't give me that honorable crap. Don't patronize me." She couldn't help jumping on that comment.

Bill didn't say anything for a moment, then quietly he said, "If that's what I did, I'm sorry. I've never had a fellow officer start crying on me."

Amy broke down completely at his words. She was a failure on all counts. Officers of the law weren't supposed to cry.

Half carrying her, he managed to get Amy out of the bathroom and back in bed. He handed her a towel. She carefully wiped her face, avoiding her wounds.

"The doctor said you're going to be fine."

"Fine." She swallowed more tears. They had to stop. "I have train tracks running down my face."

Bill ducked his head and then cleared his throat. Amy was sure she caught the sound of a chortled laugh. "The doctor didn't think that any of your wounds would leave much of a scar. They're not that deep, he said."

Amy breathed in deeply. "You don't know what it's like. You're a guy. I'm going to be marked for life."

"That's right. We guys are proud of our battle scars. Give me a break. Don't you know that women with interesting scars are intriguing? They will give you character and a mysterious appeal."

"Really?"

"I don't know. I thought it sounded good."

She hiccuped a laugh. "My face hurts."

"It's that salt water."

He pulled out a hamburger wrapped in paper and set it on the rolling table right in front of her. "I thought of getting you a beer, but decided you would have to settle for a couple sips of mine."

He pulled a bottle of Leinenkugel beer out of a paper bag and opened it, then offered it to her.

She took a long swig and felt the brew fizz down her throat. "Thank you. How'd you get this beer in here?"

"No law against alcohol in the hospital that I'm aware of. Plus, who'd ever check a cop?"

"Well, thanks. That swallow tasted good."

"Hey, we're in this together."

She looked at him: broad shoulders, brown hair, big blue eyes. Not great looking, but not bad either. "Why are you being so nice to me?"

"If you hadn't opened that door, it might have been me."

"Oh," Amy said, disappointed in his answer.

"And you're the cutest deputy in the department, train tracks and all."

"Give me that hamburger."

***

8:45 p.m.

The new morgue was under the new hospital addition that had been built a couple years ago. It was state of the art—walk-in coolers, the whole works—but Claire missed watching Dr. Lord work in the old church basement. He had retired a few years ago. He was playing as much golf as he wanted to these days. Once every few months they got together for pie. He looked better than she had ever seen him, but all he wanted to talk about was what was going on at work.

Dr. Whitaker was just starting the autopsy when Claire got to the morgue after stopping off at the sheriff's department.

"Let me just finish what I'm doing here," Dr. Whitaker said and tugged at the skin flap that was hanging loose by the chest to pull it back.

Claire watched her push body parts back into the open cavity and felt sick. Rich had still not called back with any news of Meg. The bracelet was burning a hole in her pocket.

"I'll stitch him back together after we talk." Dr. Whitaker pulled off her gloves. "Although he got a nasty bump on his head, what killed him was the knife. Whoever did it knew what they were doing. Right up under the ribs. He bled out."

"Where's the knife?"

Dr. Whitaker pointed to a rolling cart. "Over there. On that long white tray."

Claire turned and walked over to look at the knife. A boning knife about eight inches long. Chicago cutlery. It had been sharpened many times. The blade was actually thinner in the middle than it was at the end. A well-worn knife. One that looked like it belonged in somebody's kitchen.

But not her kitchen.

Claire knew where she had to go next.

CHAPTER 24

8:45 p.m.

Tammy wondered where her parents were and when they'd be back. Almost ten years old, she wasn't used to being left on her own. She tried to read, but she was too anxious

She would never forget her mother telling her about Krista.

Her mom had taken her by the arm, saying, "Honey, I have some bad news. It's about Krista." When Tammy had seen the blotchy redness of her mother's face, she knew. Her mom didn't even have to say anything. Just the word "Krista" and the look on her mother's face were enough. She knew that Krista was dead.

Now Tammy worried about everything. She knew that death could come at any moment.

Her mom and dad had told her they'd be gone for awhile, but that was before supper time. They still weren't back. She couldn't think of what they could be doing that would take them this long.

Since Krista's funeral, she knew where they often went together. But not for this long.

She made herself a grilled peanut butter and cheese sandwich. Krista and she had made the sandwich up. They called it a "Cheesenutty." Her mom thought it was gross. Tammy knew every time she made a Cheesenutty for the rest of her life she would think of her sister. It made her sad and happy at the same time.

She was sitting in her room when she looked out the window and saw the police car. She clutched her stomach and tried to be calm, but shivers ran through her. Not again. Not something bad.

Tammy tore down the stairs and out the door. A woman deputy was getting out of the car. Tammy recognized her from the morning they found Krista. She was Meg's mother.

"What happened? Where are Mom and Dad? Are they hurt?" Tammy screamed.

Claire grabbed her and said, "Everything's okay. I didn't mean to scare you. I'm sure they're fine."

Tammy pulled away. "Why are you here?"

"Do you know where your parents are?"

"Not for sure. I thought you said they're fine."

"I'm sure they're all right. I just needed to ask them a couple questions. Did you talk to them when they left?"

Tammy nodded.

"What'd they tell you?"

"They'd be gone, but not long."

"Do you have any idea where they might have gone?"

"Maybe." Tammy didn't think it was a secret.

"Tammy, I need you to tell me whatever you know."

"Well, sometimes they go someplace together after supper."

"Yeah?"

"They go visit my sister."

The woman looked puzzled, then her face cleared. "Oh, they go to the cemetery where Krista was buried?"

"Yeah." Tammy explained, "I went once, but that was enough for me. It just makes me too sad. Mom takes some flowers. Dad drives her down there. They stay for an hour or two. They miss her so much."

***

8:45 p.m.

They stopped at a Taco Bell for dinner. Arlene let Davy order a Jumbo Bean Burrito, she ordered a taco and then ate what he couldn't finish of his burrito. Once they got back in the car, Davy fell asleep, his head lolling sideways in his car seat. He didn't look very comfortable.

Arlene was sorry that the little boy wasn't sleeping in the seat next to her. She was glad that when Jared was that age he hadn't needed to sit all by himself in the backseat. She would have loved to watch Davy sleep as she drove. She could catch a glimpse of him in the rearview mirror, but she couldn't touch him.

When they were past Diamond Bluff, only a half an hour from home, Davy woke up. His head popped up and he looked around.

"Where's this?" he asked.

"We're almost home."

"At my house?"

"*My* home."

"Not my mom's?"

Arlene hated to have to remind him again that his mother was gone. A hard thing for a three-year-old to comprehend. "No, remember? We've talked about this before. She's gone far away."

Arlene could hear Davy humming a song to himself as he thought about that. She was sure she recognized the tune, but couldn't remember what it was.

"Mom coming back?"

"Remember? I told you she's gone for a long time."

"Can she see me?"

"She does see you, but you can't see her."

"Jared gone, too?"

"Just for a while. Until he gets better."

"He sick?"

"Yes, he's sick from bad medicine."

"Oh."

More humming.

Then Davy's bright voice suggested, "I know. We could sing."

"What song do you want to sing?"

"You know, that one song."

She didn't, but she played along with him. "Okay. You start."

From the back seat came Davy's small thin voice singing, "Jesus loves me this I know, for the Bible tells me so."

Arlene joined in, not believing in Jesus' love, but believing in the love and power of singing with a three-year-old boy in the night on the way home. Believing that she had taken her son to a place where he might be healed. Believing that she had done all she could do and now all that was left was to love.

"Yes, Jesus loves me. Yes, Jesus loves me. Yes, Jesus loves me. The Bible tells me so."

***

8:50 p.m.

Claire hated leaving Tammy Jorgenson home alone, but she didn't want the girl there when she talked to her parents. Claire drove to the cemetary at the corner of double J with the three big cedar trees. An old cemetery, rarely used anymore.

As she drove up she didn't see the Jorgensons there, but as she got closer she saw the Buick was tucked in behind the small cement building and the couple were sitting down on the ground on the far side of the grounds.

She parked behind their car and walked over. They both turned and looked at her, but didn't stand.

Then Emily spoke. "We're just talking to Krista. Telling her what happened."

Claire was struck by how slowly Emily was talking. Something seemed wrong. Then Roger Jorgenson tried to stand up and fell down on his knees.

The two of them were drunk. Sitting in the dark by their daughter's grave completely sloshed.

"What happened to you two?" Claire asked.

"I'll tell you everything ..." Emily started.

"Quiet, Emily," Roger said loudly, then shushed her in an exaggerated fashion.

"I can talk if I want."

"No, I'll tell her." He turned to Claire. "It was me. I did it. I was at the police station and one of the deputies told me where he was. So we went there, to that house. We walked in and he took a swing at me and then I stuck the knife in him. Is he dead?"

Claire was surprised how matter-of-fact Roger was acting. "Yes, he's quite dead."

"Good."

Claire stepped in closer to him and said, "Roger, this is serious. This is first degree murder. You might want to talk to your lawyer before you say anything else to me. Do you want me to remind you of your rights?"

"I killed the bastard. What more is there to say?"

Emily held onto her daugher's new gravestone and managed to haul herself up. "Roger, let me tell it."

Roger shushed her again.

"It's like with chickens ..." Emily began, then seemed to get lost.

Claire prompted her, "You raise chickens?"

"Yeah, every year we get a couple dozen newly hatched chicks mailed to us. The girls love it. We keep them warm in the bathroom in a big box."

"And who slaughters the chickens?"

Emily said, "I do. I can do it so fast, they never know what happened to them. I've done it all my life."

"Then you cut them up."

"Yeah, I cut them up."

"Emily, do you have a favorite knife that you use for that?"

Emily's face fell. "I do."

"Do you know where that knife is right now?"

Emily's eyes dropped and she nodded her head.

"Where?"

"He was going to kill Roger. Even though he was skinny, he was strong. He was strangling him. I couldn't let him kill my husband."

"What did you do?"

"I brought the knife with just in case. Roger didn't know I had it. I put it in my purse. Roger tried to leave without me, but I wanted to come along. I needed to know what he was going to do. I was worried about him. Roger's been crazy since Krista died."

"The knife?" Claire reminded her gently.

"Yeah, I had it in my purse. He had his hands around Roger's neck and was choking him. I took out the knife and I slid it in under his ribs."

"You knew where to put it?"

"I did. I've had a lot of practice." Emily looked down at her hands. "He was just another animal."

CHAPTER 25

9 p.m.

At the end of Jared's intake interview, Libby told him that since he had been off meth for over five days, he could go straight onto the floor. She made it sound like this was some great honor.

Jared didn't want to be on the floor, whatever that was. He didn't want to be in this rehab place at all. But his mom had left him there and paid the money so he figured he might as well go through with it.

Libby explained to him that he could leave whenever he wanted to. But the treatment center still felt like prison.

When Jared walked into his assigned room, a bearded hulk of a man sat on the edge of a twin bed, cutting his toenails. The guy had to weigh a good two hundred and fifty pounds. Obviously not into meth.

Jared knew this was the young adult section so the guy couldn't be older than twenty-five, but he looked a lot older. He even had streaks of gray in his hair.

Two twin beds were pushed to each side of the room, two dressers, and two bedside tables with alarm clocks on them. A bathroom could be seen through a door at the far end of the room.

Jared sat down on the unoccupied twin bed.

The hulk looked up and nodded. "How's it going?"

Jared didn't know what to say.

"First time?"

"What?" Jared said.

"First time in treatment?"

"Yeah."

"It's okay. It's okay. Food's not bad." The hulk flipped the toenail clippers up in the air and caught it. "What's your drug?"

"Meth."

"Tough, man. But it's possible to get out from under it."

"What's yours?" Jared asked.

"Whatever I can get my hands on, man. Whatever I can get my hands on. I've done it all. Mix it up and pour it down. That's what I say. Just pour it down."

"What do we do?"

"Whatever they tell us to. Whatever they tell us." The hulk looked him up and down. "Looks like you could use a little food. Like I said already, chow's okay here. What do I call you, dude?"

"Jared."

"Hey, Jared. Name's Duke. You can just call me Duke."

"Hi, Duke."

"Do you snore?"

"Not that I know of."

"We're going to get along fine. Long as you don't snore. Can't stand that snoring. I need my sleep. My beauty sleep." As Duke said the last line, he started to chuckle. The sound came from deep inside of him, sounding like an echo in a well. He went back to cutting his toenails.

Jared looked around the bare room. Not even a chair. Maybe that was so they would leave their rooms and socialize in the communal areas. All he wanted to do was climb under the covers and never come out.

He couldn't believe two hours ago he had a good hit of meth in his hands and that Meg had grabbed it away.

Jared thought of what happened the last time he did meth, up on the Maiden Rock with Krista and Hitch. Hitch had pulled out a few hits and offered it around. Jared had snorted up and Krista had turned it down.

But for some reason Jared had wanted Krista to try it.

He wanted her to feel the rush of the first time, the lift off, the never wanting to land again on the earth.

He told her she would love it. He told her it would make her feel like she'd never felt before: more beautiful, smarter, more powerful.

She smiled at him and said, "You sure?"

He nodded. He laid out a hit on his palm. She snorted it out of his hand. Half an hour later, she was gone.

Jared said out loud, "I think I killed someone."

Duke looked up from clipping his toenails. "I hear you, man. I hear ya."

***

9:00 p.m.

Night had settled and Meg stared at the lake stretched out below her like the darkest carpet of water. It looked possible to walk on it. Even without a drug. She felt the tinfoil package still in her hands.

She was sitting as close to the edge as she could get. There wasn't exactly an edge to the Maiden Rock. It was more like a limestone knoll that rounded over until it disappeared. Grasses and flower stalks covered the top of it. She was sitting at the edge of the grasses, her feet on the limestone. If she pushed off, she would fly out into space and then down a few hundred feet into the tops of trees, the woods at the bottom of the bluffs.

All she could see out in front of her was air and then far below the lake.

Suddenly a bird flew up the face of the bluff underneath where she was sitting and came within a few feet of her.

She knew what the bird was—a peregrine falcon. She had heard that they had started a colony here on the bluffs. The falcon soared in the updraft, the fastest bird in North America. After a few minutes, another peregrine joined the first.

Her heart lifted with them. She watched the birds roll and sway in the invisible wind that carried them along.

Suddenly, Meg was with Krista. She saw Krista thinking she was a bird, thinking she could do anything she wanted to and jumping off the rock into the sky. Meg hoped that at that moment Krista had felt complete joy, exquisite freedom. She hoped that Krista never knew fear as she plummeted to the ground, that she enjoyed her last moments of life as much as she had enjoyed all the others.

Meg watched the falcons and felt that same wind holding her up. The earth was a wonderful place to be. She was not ready to leave it.

She turned over the piece of tinfoil and watched the powder blow away. She understood as much as she could.

She didn't need to be Krista. Nor Winona, for that matter.

Laying back on the ground, Meg stared up at the sky. She had her whole life ahead of her. Why waste any of it.

"Hey," a voice said, close behind her.

She recognized the timbre of the voice. This voice had whispered in her ear and sent shivers through her bones.

She pushed herself up, turned, and saw Curt. He was standing about ten feet away, still in the trees. A bolt of happiness shot through her at the sight of him. She patted the ground next to her.

"Rich is looking for you," he said as he stepped toward her. He slipped on the grass, then caught himself. His usual awkward self. "He came to the farm and asked me where you might be."

"I'm sorry. I hope he wasn't too worried. What did you tell him?" Meg looked up at him. "How'd you find me?"

"Just a good guess. I didn't tell him you would be here because I wasn't positive. Plus, I wanted to find you myself."

"Cuz you're my soul mate," she said, falling back into their patter.

"No, I'm the soul man. Are you okay?" he asked, sinking down next to her.

Meg just pointed at the two falcons, soaring so close below them that she felt like she could almost touch their feathers, hear their wings flap, and watch their heads turn to take in their winding snake of a world.

"Why can't we be like them? Getting along like that."

"They have problems too." Curt touched her arm. "I thought you weren't talking to me?"

"Don't remind me."

Then Meg tried to explain. "I've just been so mad. I mean I've been sad, too, but I was expecting that, but the anger. I didn't know what to do with it. I felt like if I talked to you I would blow up."

"So it wasn't because of us telling Krista."

"No, it was about that too. All mixed up."

"I know how you feel." Curt paused, then continued, "I've been chopping wood for the last few days. You should try it. Swinging the axe down into a piece of wood, watching it fly apart, it gets rid of some of the guilt and anger."

"So what you're saying is who needs therapy when you can just chop wood?" Meg teased him.

"Maybe that's what's wrong with people these days—they don't do anything physical."

"Okay. I'll try it. But now we can just sit and watch the birds."

They were both quiet for a while until the falcons dropped out of sight.

"I found the guy who gave Krista the stuff," Meg said.

"You did?" Curt asked. "How? Why?"

"I got Jared to take me. He was there that night with Krista. His mom had him trapped at his house so I took Rich's truck and got him. Then we went to see that guy. I can't explain it. I had to see him."

Meg stopped for a second, remembering. But she wanted to tell Curt everything. "His name is Hitch. I felt like I needed to know what really happened. I mean, my mom's a cop. I guess I just absorbed her obsessions. You have to get to the truth. Justice and all that. I convinced Jared to take me to him. I was so mad at the crudball dealer or whatever he was. I just wanted to tell him what I thought of him. Then I saw him."

Curt waited. "And ..."

"He was awful."

"A real meth freak?"

"Yeah, gruesome. Hardly human."

"That'd be a good name for a band. Hardly Human."

"Curt, this is serious," Meg said, knowing that he was being funny because he was nervous. "It was weird. When I saw him in person I realized that there was nothing I could do to make his life worse. He had managed to find hell all by himself. I knew then that he didn't kill Krista, not really."

"He told you that?"

"No, I just knew."

"What do you mean?"

"It's so simple. He didn't kill her. No one killed Krista. Unless they actually pushed her off the bluff. Which I don't think they did. No reason to."

"Suicide?" Curt asked.

"No. I just think she felt so full of life that she thought she couldn't die. She just wanted to fly."

Curt shook his head, but didn't say anything for a moment. Then he asked, "Are you okay?"

When she had not even known where she was going herself, Curt had known where to find her. It had to mean something.

Meg took his hand and squeezed it. "I'm good."

SPECIAL THANKS

I would like to give special thanks to the West Wisconsin Land Trust for buying the 248-acre farmland which contains the Maiden Rock. It is now designated a State Natural Area and is open to the public with a hiking trail through restored prairie out to the limestone outcropping and its nesting peregrine falcons. The cover photo is courtesy of the West Wisconsin Land Trust.

Huge thanks to Bleak House Books for giving Claire and crew a home, in Wisconsin. Working with Alison and Ben is a real joy.

Many thanks always to my crew of first readers: Deborah Woodworth, Pat Boenhardt, Bill Smith, Kathy Erickson, Mary Anne Collins-Svoboda, and my trusty partner, Pete Hautman. For twenty years Pete and I have owned a small house not far from the Maiden Rock and I am still amazed at the beauty of the river, the coulees, the limestone bluffs, and the support and love of my neighbors.